THE
RUNAWAY HEIRESS

THE
RUNAWAY HEIRESS

Lillian Cheatham

A CANDLELIGHT REGENCY SPECIAL

Published by
Dell Publishing Co., Inc.
1 Dag Hammarskjold Plaza
New York, New York 10017

Dell ® TM 681510, Dell Publishing Co., Inc.

ISBN: 0-440-18083-X

Printed in the United States of America
First printing—February 1980

NOV 1980

2 hot HEAD'S CLASH
no Danger well miniscule
Little Excitment

CANDLELIGHT REGENCY SPECIAL

This book is better that I
thought it would be what
a ending the hero is a
you know what until the
last couple of pages imagine
that. Whow! It deserves
a +10 just for the ending.

CANDLELIGHT REGENCIES

CHAPTER I

It was an old-fashioned carriage of ancient lineage, painted a bright yellow, and there had apparently been some mishap to the wheel, for it was leaning drunkenly half on and half off the road. The coachman had left the leaders unattended while he bent over the wheel and ruminated on its shortcomings, so when the black stallion and its accompanying rider pounded around the corner at breakneck speed, there seemed no avoiding the coach. For a minute or two, all was pandemonium. The horse reared and screamed, with flashing hooves pawing the air, as the man attempted to keep his seat and soothe the frantic animal back onto its four feet. The job horses jerked and strained at the carriage and, following the stallion's example, squealed and fought within their traces to break free. The coachman, who had been knocked to the ground, scrambled to his feet as fast as his girth would allow him, to go to the leaders, but he reached them only seconds before the rider, who had dismounted and was holding the stallion's reins in an iron grip.

"You damn fool! What were you thinking of to allow this menace on a public road? You ought to be horsewhipped, you incompetent nincompoop!"

The danger past, the gentleman began cursing steadily and fluently, damning the collective horses, the position of the carriage, but most of all, the coachman's stupidity. Throughout it all, the elderly coachman took it in with rounded eyes and a steadily creeping expression of awe. Gradually, the gentleman's violence faded into silence, and he became aware of a commotion behind him. He turned to see the carriage's single passenger climbing out carefully, shaking her skirts and righting her bonnet, which had become more than slightly askew during the mishap.

Margaret Terrell had been frightened almost senseless when she first heard the sound of approaching hoofbeats and visualized the sort of accident that might occur on this deserted country road, miles, apparently, from the nearest habitation. Being somewhat quicker of hearing than old Danny, she was desperately trying to struggle out

8

of the carriage at the same time that he was looking up from the wheel, jaw dropping with astonishment. She had been knocked to the floor by the resultant jerking of the horses and had been given the opportunity to appreciate the colorful language that accompanied the encounter as she clambered out of the tilted carriage.

Margaret was a remarkably beautiful young woman, although at the present moment she was decidedly ruffled by her experience. She was dressed in a modish traveling costume of gray poplin trimmed with cherry red, now streaked with dirty marks. Her little gray bonnet was trimmed with a brave red feather, which had been broken and hung at a disconsolate angle. However, the gentleman noticed only that she had a quantity of dusky curls escaping from her bonnet, a retroussé nose, and a pair of the prettiest, reddest lips he had ever encountered.

Margaret was more observant. She saw that he was a tall, powerfully built gentleman with a swarthy, scowling face and gray eyes that were shadowed by overhanging black brows and lashes. A high-arched nose gave him the sinister look of a predator. He was regarding her with a mixture of apology and impatience, but he did not seem unduly embarrassed.

"I beg your pardon, madam. My language was unsuited to the presence of a lady. Are you hurt?"

9

She shook her head, aware that their carelessness might have caused a serious accident, for if he had not maintained an iron control over his high-spirited animal, there could have been a fatality to either man or beast, or both.

"I am perfectly all right," she assured him. "Since the accident was our responsibility, I think we owe you an apology."

He shrugged. He had been looking his horse over rather anxiously and now, satisfied that the animal was not harmed, he turned his attention to the carriage.

"I hope you aren't planning to go very far tonight, madam." He kicked the broken wheel with a mud-splashed boot. "It will take a while to get this repaired, and it has begun to rain again."

"Yes, I know." Margaret looked up anxiously at the lowering clouds. The mid-summer heat, which had been oppressive for the past two weeks, had broken, and it looked as though a cold, drizzling rain had settled in for a while. "I am a stranger here, sir. Can you tell me where we could find the nearest inn?"

"There's a rather primitive one further down the road," he replied disinterestedly, "a mile or two. Your coachman can find accommodations there and get the wheel repaired, but I shouldn't think it would do for you. You would be much better off seeking shelter from Queen's Keep. You may have noticed the gates to the castle when you passed them a mile or so back. Lady Maulbrais can offer you hospitality there."

Margaret had not noticed any gates, but she nodded, since the gentleman was obviously anxious to be on his way. He seemed indifferent to the weather, but then he was wearing an enveloping cloak with a number of capes that effectively shed the rain. He had already swung himself into the saddle, as though impatient to be off, and now with a slight salute of his riding crop, he was gone, leaving Margaret to cope with finding for herself a shelter at Queen's Keep.

Margaret was not unused to coping. The elderly splendor of the yellow carriage and her brave new traveling dress were misleading: the carriage was borrowed for her journey, and a new dress was a rarity for her. Had the gentleman but known it, the payment for a night's lodging at any sort of inn, primitive or not, would strain her slender resources to the utmost. She had not expected when she left Lawton Grange this morning that she would need to spend the night on the road, but she had made a late start, old Daniel had lost his way—hence, this appearance on a deserted country road—and now, the mishap to the wheel when she could ill afford the additional expense.

However, in spite of her fragile appearance, she had courage and would not allow the gentleman's indifference to her situation to daunt her. Since the death of her husband five years ago, she had learned a great deal more about the world's harshness than is normally experienced by a pretty young woman of twenty-five who is born into a leisured existence.

She and her twin sister, Teresa, had been the only children of the late squire, Sir John Stedbelow, of the village of Chedworth. He had been widowed by their birth and had not remarried, mostly through indolence, and had thereby deprived his daughters of their security, for without a brother to inherit their father's entailed estate, it went to a distant male cousin upon his death. The estate was not a large one, consisting mostly of a manor house called Oakenfield and some farmlands that had become run-down in the hands of an incompetent bailiff. As for Sir John, he had been good natured, but he was far more interested in the hunters in his stables than in the care of his land or the training of his daughters. He taught the girls to be fearless riders, but they were mothered by the vicar's wife and schooled by a harridan of a governess who believed in frequent applications of the stick and a rigorous discipline that was to serve Margaret well later, when she was forced to maintain her sister, her small son, an old nurse, and herself on a tiny income derived from her mother's dowry.

She watched wrathfully now as the horse and rider disappeared through the mist of rain. His indifference stung. He could have been more helpful, she thought resentfully, for she did not relish making her way alone to the home of a noblewoman to beg for shelter, and old Daniel was clearly inadequate to do so. So in spite of her misgivings, she directed old Daniel to go to the inn, and set out alone, on foot, for Queen's Keep.

She found the gates without any trouble. They were a pair of handsome iron gates that opened onto a long, secluded drive which in turn led to the forecourt of Queen's Keep. Until then the rain had fallen gently, but as she reached the forecourt, an ominous roll of thunder shook the ground, and the sky split apart with a jagged streak of lightning and released a torrential cloudburst. Margaret ran for the protection of the trees.

Hovering under the trees, she stared at Queen's Keep and realized that she was looking at a truly medieval castle. It was not pretty, this turreted and crenellated pile of gray-stone masonry that dated from the days of knights and their ladies. It had a grassy moat—now rapidly filling with water—surrounding it, and the drawbridge had been permanently lowered to form a driveway that led into an inner, walled courtyard. The windows, which had been enlarged to suit modern needs, were dark and lifeless behind their blank facade, and Margaret wondered if it was possible to find hospitality in such an ancient edifice.

By now, the rain had become a steady downpour and with a sigh, Margaret saw there was no hope for it but to get wet. She dashed across the moat, then the courtyard, to the broad, stone steps. The massive wooden door was opened to her hammering by an elderly butler, who was clearly astonished to find a sodden and bedraggled young woman upon the doorstep. He stepped aside to allow her to enter, and she followed him into a great hallway, high-ceilinged and somber, with wall hangings and suits of armor. Its roof was timbered with smoke-blackened beams, and the walls were gloomy with dark, ancient paneling. Beneath their feet, the floor was flagstoned, and icy with a chill that was not dispersed by a roaring fire in the enormous, yawning fireplace.

"What is the meaning of this, Judson?" The voice was cold and imperious.

It came from a lady who had emerged from one of the upstairs rooms and now stood at the top of the curving, baronial staircase. Due to the size of the great hall and its resultant gloom, Margaret could not see her face as she stammered an apology for the disturbance and attempted to explain her plight. While she talked, the woman descended but made no acknowledgment of her presence or her words. She was, Margaret saw, middle-aged, with a thin-lipped, arrogant face and skimpy gray hair. Her clothes were rich but dowdy, and as Margaret haltingly spoke, the ice-blue eyes took apart and priced the worth of everything she was wearing. Her poplin traveling suit that she had been so proud of earlier now seemed cheap and shoddy, and the frayed gloves and cracked boots were exposed in all their shabbiness.

"Can the housekeeper dry this woman's clothes for her?" she broke in rudely.

"Yes, my lady."

My lady! This, then, must be Lady Maulbrais.

"Put this woman into the back parlor and have Mrs. Parkins see to it." She turned to Margaret. "There is quite a good inn along the way. I assume that is where your coachman has gone. They will be able to put you up for the night, and as soon as your clothes are dry, you will be advised to hurry to it, for it will soon be dark."

Margaret flushed and even the butler looked uncomfortable. Shelter for a stranded traveler was mandatory; to have done less would have been to insult all precepts of decency. But there was no mention of a fire nor the simple offer of hot tea and refreshments, and she was being roughly sent on her way to an inn that she had already been assured was too primitive for a gentlewoman. Without a word, she followed the butler to a small anteroom which had no heat and was illuminated by a single candle. He said nothing, but the motherly housekeeper, Mrs. Perkins, was not as discreet as she helped Margaret remove her clinging-wet garments and wrap herself in a warm blanket.

"That is her ladyship for you. Inhospitable, that's what, and so I told that Judson when he told me about it. I'm sorry about it, ma'am, but you'll be all right at the inn. I know the innkeeper's wife personally, and she's a good sort. I'll send one of the stableboys with a message on your behalf, and he'll ask your coachman to piek you up here as soon as he can, so you won't have to walk."

Margaret answered gratefully, then asked where she was.

"You're at Queen's Keep, ma'am. It's the seat of the Earl of Maulbrais. T'was his mother you saw. Lady Serena Maulbrais, the Dowager Countess. The Earl is generous enough, but her ladyship has always been mean when it comes to extending hospitality to strangers. But there, you will be all right. I'll have your clothes soon dried by the kitchen fire, and I'll send along some tea, even though t'wasn't ordered!" she added defiantly.

Margaret had to smile at the thin little creature who brought her tea. She was not wearing a uniform, and the short sleeves of her muslin dress showed an unattractive expanse of goose-pimpled arms. She was apparently some sort of upper-class servant since she did not hurry away to other duties but lingered to talk.

"I hope you don't get in trouble with her lady-ship. She didn't order tea, you know." Margaret sipped the hot tea appreciatively.

The girl smiled and shook her head. She was un-fortunately possessed of an oversized nose and a wide mouth crowded with crooked teeth. Cork-screw, blond curls framed her little face, although its piquancy and that flashing smile saved her from being distressingly plain. Margaret wondered about her age since those curls and the childish dress made her look about twelve years old, but she was not shy about asking questions.

"Surely you aren't going out into that rain and attempt to drive on tonight?"

Margaret wondered what other course was open to her if she did not avail herself of the inn, but she explained cheerfully that she would stay there tonight.

"Is it primitive?" she added.

"You will be all right," the girl replied evasively. "You will be the only woman, I am sure, but the innkeeper's wife will see to your safety. They have no private parlor, so you will have to eat your meals in your room, but it is cheap and the bed will be clean."

Margaret reflected that this, at least, was not un-desirable. Evidently it had not occurred to the man who rode the black stallion that money might be an object. She thought of asking the girl if she knew him, but did not.

"Have you come from a distance? Where are you going?" the girl asked eagerly.

Margaret smiled at her curiosity. "I haven't come from far away. I live in Chedworth, and have been visiting for the past week at Lawton Grange. It is a hospital near Bath. Do you know of it?"

The girl shook her head.

"It belongs to a surgeon called Dr. Stockton. He was a gentleman who inherited a fine estate and quite a lot of money. Instead of using his money on himself, he became a physician and now uses it to help other people. Lawton Grange is his home, which he has converted into a hospital."

"What a strange man he must be."

Margaret smiled. "Not so strange. Merely a kind, good man who cannot ignore the sufferings of the sick and wretched, and does something about it. He has received a great deal of censure from his neighbors, who disapprove of a hospital nearby." And of the poor, mad creatures who inhabit the hospital, Margaret added silently. "He kindly lent me his carriage for the trip."

"Are you in love with him?"

Margaret laughed. "Of course not, you funny little thing. One doesn't fall in love with a gentleman merely because he is kind." The fleeting image of a scowling, black-browed brute who was definitely *not* kind flashed unbidden through her mind. "My sister, Teresa, is a patient in his hospital. I do not get to visit her very often, and when I do, Dr. Stockton insists that I must stay at least a week. He thinks my visits are good for her. This morning, when I was ready to leave, he offered me the carriage that belonged to his parents. It had been stored in the carriage house for a long time, and I think some of the timbers had weakened, because the wheel broke—" she stopped, wondering if this young girl who was listening to her so intently was really interested in the story of her mishap on the road. She wondered, too, if the girl would be shocked to learn that Dr. Stockton's hospital was for the benefit of mental patients and that he was renowned throughout the world for his treatment of mental diseases, commanding large fees for his services. Would she be horrified to learn that Teresa, whom she had mentioned so casually, would be in Bedlam right now if he had not consented to take her as a patient? What was she really thinking as she watched Margaret with an odd, faraway look in her eyes?

Apparently, like most young girls her age, her mind was dwelling on romance, having noticed Margaret's wedding ring. "Will your husband be waiting for you?"

Margaret felt a twinge of irritation at the unabashed curiosity and knew that she should not be encouraged. She wondered again who she might be. The governess, surely, if not an upper-level housemaid. Her manners and voice were cultured, although her impertinent questions were outrageous.

"My husband is dead," she replied coolly. "He died five years ago, when my little son, Jodie, was a baby. Jodie and my old nurse live at home with me. *They* will be waiting for me." And that, my girl, is my life in a nutshell, she could have added.

The girl was no fool. She reddened slightly at the reproof and rose at once with the tray.

"Please, you will take my advice about the inn?" she asked anxiously. "Promise me that you will stay there tonight."

Margaret shrugged. "I have no choice but to do so, my dear. I only hope Daniel is able to get the wheel repaired tonight so that we can make an early start tomorrow."

Later that night, as she prepared for bed, Margaret wondered again at the girl's insistence. She had been correct in her assurances about the inn's respectability. It had been dingy and lacked a private dining room, but the bed had been aired and the innkeeper's wife had personally seen to her comfort and her supper. Margaret had followed her suggestion to bolt her bedroom door, but she was not disturbed, although the sounds of revelry from the public room downstairs floated upward long after she went to bed.

Margaret did not dream, but as she drifted on the fringe of sleep, she thought again of the stranger who had disapproved of the inn and she wondered who he might be. He had known about Queen's Keep, but obviously he had not known Lady Maulbrais very well.

CHAPTER II

As a matter of fact, Marcus Salterson knew Lady Maulbrais very well indeed; but he had never plumbed the depths of her snobbery and contempt, perhaps because he had never been in the unenviable position of one whom she considered her inferior. He had not been long departed from Queen's Keep and a rancorous session with Lady Maulbrais when he had the near-fatal collision with Dr. Stockton's carriage. Some of the acerbity he subsequently displayed might be excused for that reason, although he had been sincere when he assured Margaret that she would be welcomed by her ladyship.

Actually, Mr. Salterson stood in a peculiar position in relation to Lady Maulbrais. For eighteen years he had been forced to acknowledge a family connection with her that he found as irritating as a canker sore on one's tongue, ever since his sister Amelia saw fit to marry into the noble Maulbrais family. For the past twelve years, since Amelia's death, he had shared with Lady Maulbrais the guardianship of their niece, the result of the union between Amelia and Rodney, younger brother of the late Earl of Maulbrais. Now, all three were dead, Amelia, Rodney, and the Earl, and Mr. Salterson found himself frequently engaged in a tug-of-war with the Earl's widow over the terms of Annabelle's guardianship. It was a condition that he found barely supportable, since only by throttling his temper and preserving a bland demeanor could he endure the proximity at all.

The day of the accident, he had been summoned to Queen's Keep, which he privately regarded as a moldering pile of stones, by a letter from her ladyship, and the tone seemed urgent enough for him to put aside his ingrained dislike of ever having to set foot inside the place. It had been a twenty-mile horseback ride through rain squalls to an interview that he would much rather have consigned to the devil. As he handed his cloak to Judson, he tried to read in that worthy's face an indication of what quarter the wind might be blowing from, but predictably, Judson gave nothing away.

However, when he was ushered into the Yellow Salon to find that both Francis Cedric St. Germain Audrey Herenford, the sixth Earl of Maulbrais, and his mother were awaiting him, Mr. Salterson's temper rapidly worsened. Her ladyship's letter had informed him that Annabelle, his niece, was to be the subject of discussion, but since she was not present and Cedric was, he could be certain that this was to be yet another wrangle over money.

However, Lady Serena Maulbrais surprised him. Wearing what passed for a smile on her thin, vinegary face, she announced that Annabelle had accepted her cousin Cedric's proposal of marriage. Mr. Salterson's face remained impassive, but he was conscious of a small shock of disbelief, not at the betrothal, which he had considered a foregone conclusion, but at the news that Cedric had been willing to propose. As for his niece, he would have thought her too young. True, she had had a London season, one that had woefully betrayed her shortcomings, but if the chit wished to be married, who was he to cavil? His responsibility lay with the guardianship of her fortune, and on that head, he was grimly determined to do battle with the avaricious element of the Herenford family in the person of the dowager, Lady Maulbrais.

"Of course, this will mean that the allowance of a school girl will no longer be sufficient for dear

Annabelle?" Lady Maulbrais looked at him inquiringly.

Since Annabelle's allowance, even in her infancy, had never been anything like that of a schoolgirl, Mr. Salterson merely nodded.

"Actually, by the terms of the will, her fortune should pass into her husband's hands." Mr. Salterson waited, aware that Lady Maulbrais knew the terms of his sister's will even better than he did himself. "Subject to your approval of her choice, of course." Her ladyship modified her statement when Mr. Salterson's silence grew overlong. "Cedric is prepared to take your responsibility off your hands."

Mr. Salterson looked at the Earl, who seemed prepared to allow his mother to speak for him. At twenty-six, he was hardly a callow youth, yet he betrayed his nervousness in the way he tugged his wilting shirt-points and refused to meet Mr. Salterson's eyes. Far better his mother, thought Mr. Salterson cynically; she at least had the courage of her convictions. Cedric had burst upon the fashionable London scene some years before and proceeded to outdo the record left by his illustrious parent for reckless expenditure and riotous living. He was very like his father in looks, too, having the Herenford chin and startling blue eyes. But he was a gamester. He never missed a horse race or a boxing match if they were within the distance of a day's journey. On those occasions, he could be found at the betting table, aroused to fever pitch. Mr. Salterson, who had occasionally seen him at such spectacles, had observed in him the signs of a dedicated gambler and marveled that he had nothing of his mother's cold, cautious nature, although so far as he could see, his weakness and vanity had nothing to do with viciousness, but were the result of improper training instilled in him by an overindulgent mother.

"I am to gather, then," Mr. Salterson said sardonically, "that Lord Maulbrais is not expecting to support his wife?"

Cedric wriggled, but his mother spoke up sharply. "Don't be absurd, Salterson! You know that we are dependent upon Annabelle's income! And once they are married, their expenditures will rise. I should not have to tell you that!"

"You don't. I am prepared to adjust it accordingly."

"I called you here today merely to ask for a sizable advance for bridal expenses. I realize that it will have to come out of her capital, but the circumstances are unusual. Three or four, perhaps five thousand pounds will be enough——"

"Have the bridal bills sent directly to me," Mr. Salterson broke in. "I will pay them as they come in."

"I prefer having the money in hand," her ladyship said angrily. "I must say, Salterson, I did not expect you to be *mean* about this."

"I am prepared to adjust my niece's income, madam, but not yours," he said smoothly. "I won't back away from plain speaking, but it cannot be any surprise to either of you that I don't consider Lord Maulbrais a competent person to handle Annabelle's estate. Speaking without roundabation, I don't trust him, in fact. His follies in town have left me with a poor opinion of his intentions as well as his good sense."

This was plain speaking with a vengeance. Lady Maulbrais blinked. "Cedric will not be allowed to handle any of it," she promised grudgingly. "*I* will do that."

Mr. Salterson shook his head. "That means nothing to me, madam. You are incapable of denying him anything he asks for. Do you think I don't know why you want such a sum of money in a hurry? Why good God, madam, the whole town knows that he fled just ahead of the bailiff!"

The Earl leaped to his feet. "How dare you, sir? You have no right——"

"Sit down, Lord Maulbrais," Mr. Salterson said in a bored voice. "When you lend yourself to some trumpery tale of bridal fees in an attempt to gouge five thousand pounds from me, you give me the right to say anything I like to you. I know precisely what your debts are, down to the last halfpenny, including what you owe to your tailor and your wine merchant."

"I should have known that in the end you must be vulgar," Lady Maulbrais said coldly. "A gentleman would not lend himself to such prying curiosity."

Mr. Salterson grinned, momentarily softening the hard outlines of his thin, dark face. "But I am vulgar, ma'am," he said promptly. "Vulgar—and curious—and rich. And I know exactly where my own money goes, so why should I do less for my niece? Meanwhile, talk to your man of business. I'll meet with him whenever he wishes to see to the marriage settlements. But I will not anticipate them to bail your son out of his predicament."

Lady Maulbrais eyed him sourly. He was hard, was Marcus Salterson, and she was beating against a granite rock in an attempt to change his mind. He had not been at all discomposed by her spiteful remark, and spiteful it had been; for she, at least, knew that his birth was impeccable, else her husband, even with her accompanying fortune, would never have allowed his younger brother to marry Amelia Salterson. As for the fortune, she might admit to herself that it was Salterson money that kept the wolf from the Herenford castle door, but it lowered her pride to admit it to him. Actually, she had gotten into the habit of thinking of

Amelia's money as her own and Cedric's, and she considered it outrageous for Marcus Salterson to insist on following the legal terminology of the will. It would seem to her that the intent was what one must bear in mind, and God knows, dear Amelia had meant for her money to eventually come to Cedric. Had it not been Amelia herself who, bending over Annabelle's cradle, had said, "Someday, Serena, she must marry Cedric,"? And from then on, it had been understood. If Amelia had lived, Cedric would not now be living in penury, forced to flee town to avoid his tailor and wine merchant, forced to sell off unencumbered bits of the estate to pay his gaming debts. Amelia, when she had made that will, had never intended for her own brother to jealously keep from Cedric what was rightfully his.

It was all the fault of that will, she said aloud, that will that placed Annabelle's eighty thousand pounds in the hands of her uncle Marcus until she was twenty-five—and in fact, forever, if he was not satisfied with her choice of a husband. Amelia had been more fond of her husband's family than of her own brother, but she had unfortunately preferred him when it came to the guardianship of her fortune. Hard Salterson common sense had made the decision for her. Hard, hard.

"If she had not," Mr. Salterson replied calmly to the bitter words she had spoken aloud, "there would have been nothing left by now. Come, madam," he added sharply, "I am weary of this talk. You shan't budge me from my position! Be satisfied with what you have. I am open to any reasonable request once the marriage takes place. But Annabelle is only seventeen, and I shan't see her made a pauper before she is twenty-one!"

To himself, he sounded like a reasonable, persuadable man, but he saw that her ladyship had not yielded one hostile inch. God, she was a stupid woman, Marcus Salterson thought with a sigh. Whatever had possessed Amelia to consider this woman a fit guardian for her child? She should have anticipated that Maulbrais faced an early demise, given his fondness for food and drink. Left in charge, Serena Maulbrais had ridden him hard ever since, fighting for every farthing she could squeeze from him. Selfish and greedy and, he suspected, entirely too careless of Annabelle's welfare. She had not even bothered to dress the child properly, so that her first season had been a total disaster. He was the first to admit that Annabelle was no beauty, having inherited the Salterson nose as well as her father's eyes and chin, but to dress her in blinding pink or that startling shade of aquamarine-blue, with those flaxen ringlets, had been to make her look like an insipid, waxen doll. That, plus the chirping "Yes, sirs" and "No, sirs" that were her only contribution to any conversation, had made Mr. Salterson wonder uncomfortably if she might not be slightly simple. It had been enough to throw off all but the most determined fortune hunter, and Annabelle's unnerving habit of staring blankly with her mouth agape had done the rest. She could count herself fortunate, he thought cynically, that Cedric was there to fall back on, no matter what his motive.

He would have been chagrined to know that for once, Lady Maulbrais agreed with him. She had sent for Marcus Salterson ostensibly to inform him of the approaching nuptials, but also in hopes of persuading him to anticipate the marriage by relieving Cedric of some of his most pressing debts. She had seen at once that it would be useless, although one would think he would be grateful to have Cedric even consider Annabelle. Why, the child was an antidote, and nothing would ever bring her up to Herenford standards as a future chatelaine of Queen's Keep. It was her common Salterson blood, no doubt, of which the man opposite her had more than his share. He also had the gray eyes, the determined chin, and the high-bridged, aquiline nose that reminded her of her sister-in-law. How unfortunate that what made up for attractiveness in a male was hideous in a female.

Serena Maulbrais had known Marcus Salterson since he was a fifteen-year-old schoolboy, and she had never liked him. Unfortunately, with his birth (his mother was the daughter of a duke, and his father had equally noble connections) and the Salterson gold, he had not needed her approval for his entry into society. All doors were open to him. He frequently set people's backs up with his careless manners, but because he was a Salterson, it was overlooked. His presence was sought by every hostess in London, and he was the goal of every matchmaking mama. However, at thirty-five, Marcus Salterson seemed to be a permanent bachelor, preferring to purchase his pleasures directly from the Cyprian set. Occasionally, Lady Maulbrais allowed herself rosy visions of the future, with his fortune coming to her by way of Annabelle or a grandchild, but she knew that he was perfectly capable of marrying just for spite to prevent even so much as a sixpence from falling into Herenford hands.

He did not even have the decency to dress properly while calling on a lady, she thought peevishly. What other man but Salterson would show up in a drawing room wearing a loudly checked waistcoat, leather breeches, and topboots liberally splashed with mud? From the spurs set into his heels, she judged that he had ridden horseback all the way from town, like a lackey following his master's carriage. She was thankful that Cedric had no interest in emulating the Salterson set, which was given over to hard sports, hard drinking, and deep gaming. She had heard of horse races or boxing matches among its participants, merely for the pleasure of testing one's skill with the ribbons or in the ring, with thousands of pounds wagered on the outcome. Lady Maulbrais would have enjoyed hearing of the loss of some of Mr. Salterson's pounds, but like all persons who could afford to lose, he invariably won.

As a matter of fact, Mr. Salterson had not ridden all the way from town, but from a friend's hunting lodge twenty miles to the north. He had been enjoying a well-earned rest with friends when a rider from his town house brought down the week's accumulation of mail. It did not occur to him to consider Lady Maulbrais's sensibilities, nor would he have cared if they were offended, when he decided to ride cross-country by trying out Lord Carlyle's black stallion, which he was considering buying for himself.

Feeling that he had successfully concluded the day's business, he rose and prepared to take his leave. He felt that he had endured a great deal today, with all the brangling and a meager, lukewarm tea, and his present mood did not augur well for the ride back through the rain.

"Do you not wish to speak to your niece?" Lady Maulbrais asked dryly.

Frankly, no, he did not. He had no idea what to

say to the chit, for he was not at his best with very young ladies. Usually, he patted her cheek and muttered some inanity, but he was too cross at the present to put himself through any more strain; so mendaciously announcing that he regretted exceedingly having no time for her today, he took his leave.

He was directed to the carriage entrance, where his horse was saddled and awaiting him. As he stepped outside, he looked back and up at Queen's Keep. An enormous pile of gray masonry erected by the first baron, Francis de Maulbrais, in the fourteenth century, it had descended in a direct line to the present lord, who was certainly an inadequate keeper of the flame. Mr. Salterson felt a twinge of pure regret for Cedric's spinelessness and that he was too occupied in wringing every groat he could out of the estate for his own amusement rather than wasting it on his hereditary obligations.

As he swung himself into the saddle and sniffed the damp, crisp air, he noticed that a small, cloaked figure had followed him and was waiting in the doorway. Annabelle. He was unexpectedly touched with a fleeting remorse at the sight of the small, white face. She had apparently expected to see him. Calling her to him, he leaned forward and ruffled her curls, pinched her cheeks, and feeling positively avuncular, asked her jocularly what she would like for a wedding present. He was surprised by her reaction. She glared at him fiercely, then without a word, whirled around and flew back inside. What ailed the brat? He had done his duty. He shrugged slightly, and with relief, wheeled the stallion toward the gates, where he could set the pace at a fast, bruising gallop and blow the distaste he had felt during the past hour out of his head. At the same time, he was guiltily conscious that he had, somehow, disappointed Annabelle.

His pace was too fast for an open road. He was aware of that before the accident happened. It was his fault that he almost came to a bad end when he met the yellow carriage. The fluency of his curses had been due to the relief he felt when he discovered that he had not caused an injury or, even worse, a death. He had been rather regretful that he had had to leave the attractive young woman by the roadside, for under any other circumstances he would have been tempted to further her acqaintance. But the threatening weather, the difficulty in controlling the skittish animal between his knees, and the late hour all combined to make him decide to hurry on; and he soon forgot her, since Lord Carlyle's house party included women, and among them the beautful and temperamental actress whom Mr. Salterson had lately taken into his keeping.

* * *

Meanwhile, Margaret Terrell, although she might dream of a gentleman on a black horse, was not so foolish as to daydream of him the following day. In fact, the following morning's events chased him completely out of her mind, as she learned why the girl at Queen's Keep had been so insistent that she go to the inn. After breakfast, as the old coach lumbered up the lane and out of sight of the inn, she was waiting for them. A portmanteau rested at her feet, and she was wearing a shabby cloak much too long for her, with a hood that ruthlessly flattened her flaxen curls.

Margaret was a tender-hearted girl and had known adversity too well herself not to sympathize with distress in others, and when that distress was caused by Lady Maulbrais, her partisanship was aroused. Already prepared to believe the worst of her ladyship, her heart swelled with indignation as she learned how the disagreeable woman had cruelly turned off this child without even a reference, merely because she learned that she had carried a tea tray to Margaret without permission.

Susan Plunkett admitted that she was the governess, just as Margaret had thought. "When her ladyship said that I must be gone by daylight, I thought of you," she said tearfully, her big eyes beseeching Margaret. "My family lives beyond London, and since Chedworth is on the way, I hoped you would allow me to ride with you that far, ma'am?"

Margaret could not refuse. In fact, she thought indignantly, only the hardest of hearts would forget the child's tender years. Eagerly, she offered Susan a bed for the night, so that she could resume her trip to London after a good night's sleep.

Susan turned out to have unexpected qualities. She was no stammering little miss, and once she got over her first shyness, she was an articulate, even amusing, companion, keeping Margaret entertained throughout the day with a fund of stories about Queen's Keep, its occupants, and the titled visitors who stayed there from time to time. From Lady Maulbrais down to the 'tweeny maid, they all came in for their share of ridicule, but in particular she had some discreditable stories about Lady Maulbrais's son, the Earl. Margaret, whose social circle had never gone much beyond the confines of Chedworth, was amused to learn that an Earl could stammer, have spots, and squeeze the housemaids behind the doors. She knew she ought not to encourage Susan to talk about her former employers; nevertheless, she could not resist hearing about the exalted beings who inhabited a world totally unlike her own. It was disconcerting to learn that this child knew it better than she did.

The rain continued to fall throughout the day, slowing their progress. Daniel, who was on loan from Dr. Stockton, saw no reason to push the horses beyond their capabilities, so by the time they arrived in Chedworth, it was late afternoon. Due to the rain obscuring her vision, Susan did not see anything of the village they passed through until they stopped before a picket fence bearing a sign that was lettered MULBERRY COTTAGE. Dimly, Susan made out the small, huddled shape of a cottage with dormer windows and a thatched roof. A candle shone in the front window. The wheels had hardly rolled to a stop before the door was flung open, spilling candlelight out onto the garden path, and a small, excited boy flew out the door and flung himself into Margaret's arms. Susan followed more slowly, suddenly shy about her position as an overnight house guest.

Polly, Margaret's old nurse, was waiting for them, and she beamed hospitably when Susan was introduced to her and little Jodie. As they waited in the small entrance hall for Daniel to bring in their luggage, Susan looked around surreptitiously. The little cottage would have fit comfortably into the Grand Hall of Queen's Keep. There was a kitchen and a parlor downstairs, with a set of narrow, box stairs from the hall leading up to three small bedrooms. One, the nursery, Margaret told her laughingly, had been fashioned apparently from a cupboard. But the single impression Susan gained was one of coziness and cleanliness, for the simple pieces of furniture gleamed with a patina of beeswax, the floors were shining, and there was a fresh, clean smell throughout the house. A copper bowl glowing with red poppies had been placed on the chest in the hall and caught the gleam of candlelight. In the diminutive parlor, a round table had been covered with a tablecloth and set with blue cottage dishes for supper.

Altogether Susan felt like a little girl in a doll house. Except that this was not a doll house; it was a real one, and the three people who lived here were real and prepared to hospitably add a fourth to its cramped space.

Supper was served early so that Jodie could be put to bed, but by then he no longer wanted to leave Susan. Margaret finally had to carry an over-excited, exhausted little boy to bed, kicking and screaming, leaving Susan in the kitchen playing with Jodie's puppy, which had been recently added to the household and was still not house-broken. Margaret herself was tired, and she wanted nothing so much as to put Jodie to sleep and then retire early herself. However, it was not to be. As she was coming out of Jodie's nursery, after an extralong bedtime story, Polly beckoned to her from the room the guest was sharing with Margaret.

"Miss Meg. I couldn't help seeing it. When I went in to turn down the coverlet, it was there in plain sight. The silly girl had made no attempt to hide it."

"It" was a jewelry case that had been left on the bed, along with a few articles of clothing scattered about with all the careless disdain of one who had never had to pick up after herself. The box was inlaid with mother-of-pearl and had gold hasps and locks, and Margaret saw that it was extremely valuable in itself. She raised the lid cautiously. It was filled with jewelry piled carelessly in a heap; lustrous pearls, glowing with an almost translucent sheen, tangled with glittering diamonds and the green fire of emeralds.

"It's real, Miss Meg!" Yes, thought Meg stupidly, there was no need for Polly to state the obvious. When one saw the real thing, there was no mistaking it. "What kind of girl have you brought home? Is she a—thief? If she is, you must get her out before she involves you in her crime!"

"I am *not* a thief!" Susan's voice was shrill with indignation. She was standing in the doorway, fists clenched. "It all belongs to me! I haven't stolen any jewelry! And I wasn't going to leave it behind for Aunt Serena to keep!"

"Who are you, Susan?" Margaret asked sternly. "Don't try to pretend that you are a penniless governess, not after—this. You have a fortune here in gems. Who is this Aunt Serena? I want the truth!"

Susan burst into tears and flung herself at Margaret, whose arms automatically closed around her. "I—I am Annabelle Herenford, Mrs. Terrell! Lady Maulbrais is my aunt. I have run away from her because she is so wicked and cruel, and oh, I am so unhappy! Please, please don't send me back," she pleaded.

Margaret patted the thin, shaking shoulders. "Of course, dear, of course I won't send you back," she said soothingly, without any clear idea of what she was promising.

CHAPTER III

Margaret Terrell knew very well that she was wrong in encouraging Annabelle to believe that she would give her sanctuary. The law was clear on the subject of runaways, and in Annabelle's case, there had obviously been no cruel mistreatment, no beating, no being locked away while fed on bread and water, nor any of the other fabled happenings that one associated with a castle like Queen's Keep, with its own moat and dungeons. What was more, the child had fled carrying a fortune in gems. No matter how sorry one might be for her, anyone harboring her would be subject to the strictest penalty of the law if, for instance, the Bow Street runners tracked the runaway to her present whereabouts and discovered that she had been given a haven for any longer than it took to notify her legal guardians.

But Margaret was incapable of saying no. As a girl, she had never been one to consider the consequences when embarking upon a course of action that might seem foolish or ill-advised to others. The old tabbies of Chedworth and the neighboring village of Little Mitford, who had had a scandal-broth brewing about Margaret Stedbelow at various times throughout most of her twenty-five years of life, could have told a thing or two about her impulsiveness; it had been getting her into scrapes since she was out of leading strings. She had been the despair of her governess, Miss Prouder, who used to inform her special friends, Miss Duckworth and Mrs. Millington, that Margaret Stedbelow, although possessing a soft heart, was nevertheless headed toward disaster if she continued to allow it to rule her head. "A deplorable tendency to leap before she looks" was the way she had put it.

Proudie's old friends considered that the new Margaret had mellowed somewhat since her marriage; as for Miss Prouder, now governess to the snobbish daughters of a rich industrialist in the north of England, she would have said unhesitatingly that Margaret Stedbelow would never change. The vicar's wife and Polly, too, knew that her docile facade hid a reckless, fiery nature. In spite of the sobering circumstances of her widowhood, Margaret was still the same hoyden who had once waded, arms flailing, into a gang of village children who were taunting Teresa. It was that recklessness that worried Polly as she made an effort to appeal to Margaret's common sense the following morning.

"You can't afford the trouble, Miss Meg. You've got to think of yourself and Master Jodie. Write to Miss Annabelle's guardian letting her know where she is. You have enough trouble of your own without taking on that girl's, too."

Of course, Margaret knew that Polly was right. She could not afford the trouble. She could not even afford to keep Annabelle with her, for it was only by dint of the most stringent economy and of Dr. Stockton's cutting his fees to the bone that she was able to keep Teresa in his hospital, in a clean, bright room instead of a crowded cell in Bedlam. Somehow, Annabelle reminded her of Teresa. Perhaps it was the circumstances, for Teresa had desperately needed her help too. Or perhaps it was Annabelle's eyes and that wistful little face that reminded one of a solemn monkey.

Polly would have scoffed to think a self-willed little heiress like Annabelle Herenford could remind anyone of gentle Teresa. Privately, Polly thought Annabelle was a young woman who would always land on her feet. She was rich and belonged to a noble family, and Polly darkly suspected that she had taken advantage of Margaret's sweet nature for her own selfish ends. In her opinion, Annabelle was as tough as an old shoe, as flinty as any of her hard-nosed old Norman ancestors, who had certainly been brigands and thieves when they crossed the Channel and made mincemeat of their enemies.

And upstairs, reposing casually in a drawer, was a king's ransom in jewels! To Polly, that spoke of the arrogance of wealth. She had always observed that rich people were quick to make accusations, and she could not see them accepting this loss tamely, without calling out the full resources of the law. No, nor of blaming Miss Meg, either, no matter how innocent she was. When the time came to apportion the blame, Polly somehow doubted if Annabelle would receive her share of it. And if Polly knew anything of noble families, they would be very anxious to hush up any gossip concerning their ward. A girl who had run away from home and spent some time in a country cottage with strangers, miles from those who knew her, would be damaged goods in the marriage mart. And what better way of making sure that no unsavory story leaked out than to clap the only witness to such goings-on into prison, branded as a thief? Who would help her Miss Meg then? She had no one! Oh, yes, Polly could see it all clearly. It was her beloved nursling who could not see what stared her in the face.

It was therefore a militant and anxious old woman who confronted Margaret at breakfast, pouring out her fears. Margaret set about trying to soothe her.

"I will admit that everything you say is true, Polly, but I promise you it won't come to that. I will see that her guardian is notified, but first I must learn what has driven her to such desperate measures. Until I do, I cannot desert this girl. I suggested writing to her guardian last night as you suggest, but she became almost hysterical. I had to promise that I would do nothing until she had a chance to talk to me again. When she awakens, we will both listen to her story, and you may air your views then. Afterwards, together we will persuade her to approach her aunt in a sensible fashion. Surely Lady Maulbrais will be glad to hear that she is safe. After all, it is sheer luck that she fell in with me instead of some unprincipled person who might take advantage of her innocence. I am sure her aunt will be so relieved to have her back safe and sound that she will forgive her for everything."

Polly was slightly mollified. "All right, Miss

Meg, we'll wait, if you say so," she agreed reluctantly. "But you must think of yourself and the boy. He would have no one but me if you were sent to prison, for Miss Teresa is not able to——"

"Nonsense, Polly, I am not going to prison! Don't be absurd," Margaret said bracingly. "I am far more likely to be overwhelmed with thanks and gratitude from her guardian! Although," she added thoughtfully, "I must say, after having met her ladyship, I would hate to be under her domination. Last night Annabelle was talking rather wildly, and she said that she must break from her aunt or be doomed forever. I suppose the poor child thinks she may never marry and have a home of her own. And frankly, if she doesn't do something about her clothes and herself, she may well be right. You should see that wardrobe, Polly! Not a garment costing less than twenty pounds and most of them far more, I should think; yet, all are the most hideous colors—one a bright, angry pink, which with her high color and yellow hair must be a distressing combination for her! Why doesn't her aunt employ a competent dressmaker? And an abigail who would do something about those frizzy curls? While she is here, I intend to see if I can't steer her gently toward some suitable clothes and a new hair style."

Polly was appalled at those large-minded plans,

which seemed to imply that Annabelle's stay might be a lengthy one, but she managed to laugh as though Margaret were making a funny joke.

"Now, Miss Meg, she won't be staying long enough for that! You'll not be telling me she ran away from home because she wanted new clothes, are you?"

Margaret flushed. "No, of course not. Her aunt——"

"Her aunt, Miss Meg, in spite of her ill-bred manner toward you, has given Miss Annabelle a great deal of cosseting, some costly clothes and rich jewels, and yet, she suddenly decided to leave home. Why? Was it a whim, or what? Did she listen to you, Miss Meg, and childlike, get a sudden desire to go a-traveling? Don't you see, child, that's what those relatives of hers will say?"

Margaret said nothing. Polly's words were making her more than ever aware of her shortcomings in not finding out more about her house guest. "I wouldn't let her tell me anything last night," she said defensively. "She was so tired——" Tired? Or clever enough to evade questions by pretending tiredness, Margaret wondered uncomfortably.

Annabelle found it a strange experience to awaken to an empty room, without a maid to draw the curtains or present her with an early morning cup of chocolate. She had never been a slugabed type of person, so did not lie until nearly noon as her cousin Cedric, for instance, was wont to do when he came down from London. But she had never dressed herself nor combed her own hair, and she stared at the rumpled bed, perplexed, conscious of a hopeful desire to smooth it down, but without the slightest notion of how to go about it.

When she got downstairs after having, with much difficulty, dressed herself, she was feeling amazingly well and knew none of the cares that were weighing upon Polly and Margaret. One look at their faces, however, told her that they had been talking about her, and she could guess how the conversation had run. She was struck with remorse at the worried look in Margaret's eyes when they met hers.

She seated herself at the kitchen table and said in a rush, "Indeed, I have thrust myself upon you in such a fashion, without an explanation, that it is a wonder that you don't throw me out of the door and tell me to be on my way! I know I lied to you and used you and now am asking you to be further forbearing, and I know just what a quandary I am placing you in, Mrs. Terrell, but oh, please don't be angry with me! I couldn't bear for you to turn your back on me too!"

Margaret's face lightened considerably, and even Polly looked less forbidding. Annabelle's frank capitulation had won where a more studied appeal would have been suspect.

"Of course I don't intend to turn my back on you, my dear," Margaret said warmly, "but you must be frank with me. However, first you must breakfast, for I am sure you are hungry."

"Not a morsel shall pass my lips until I have told you my story," Annabelle replied sternly. "It would be taking food under false pretenses."

Polly, who was inclined to agree with her, nevertheless grimly poured her a glass of milk and placed a plate of scones filled with stiff, rich, country jam before her. The aroma was irresistible, and Annabelle was soon making a hearty breakfast.

"Mrs. Terrell——" she began, her mouth full.

"First, don't call me Mrs. Terrell," Margaret said firmly. "Call me Margaret, or better still, Meg, as most of my friends do. Now, why did you say 'turn your back on me too'?" she asked curiously. "Have you appealed to someone else to rescue you from your aunt and been refused?"

"My uncle Marcus might have helped me had he not been so selfishly involved in his own affairs," Annabelle, her mouth rimmed with a milk moustache, replied. "I did not appeal to him, for I knew it was useless, but he is the only person who could have helped me escape from Cedric. He has never concerned himself with me, however, even when I was in London, where he could have seen me occasionally. He considers me bothersome and an unpleasant duty."

"Good heavens, what a disagreeable person he must be if that is true! But I cannot believe—— Who told you such a wicked thing?"

"My cousin Cedric," Annabelle replied simply. "But I knew it was true when I saw how readily he agreed to my marrying Cedric."

"Marrying Cedric!" Margaret gasped. "Is that what this is all about? Is that why you——"

"Yes, of course," Annabelle said surprisingly. "I ran away so that I would not have to marry my odious cousin Cedric, who is a little worm and who doesn't like me any more than I like him. And I warn you, Meg, if you force me to return home and marry him, I—I—I'll kill myself!"

"For shame!" snapped Polly. "You're a wicked girl to suggest such a thing! If you don't wish to marry your cousin, why don't you merely say so?"

"I did. I begged and begged, and my aunt would not listen to me. I thought surely my uncle Marcus would help me, but he would not interfere and——"

"Wait. Let's go back to the beginning," Margaret begged. "Tell me, who is your uncle Marcus? Is he related to your mother? Her brother? But he——"

"He is Marcus Salterson. My mother was Amelia Salterson," Annabelle explained, as though that was the answer to everything. When her audience did not seem to be impressed, she added hopefully, "She was an heiress, you see, when she married my father and saved the Herenford family from ruin. She had a fortune of eighty thousand pounds, but my uncle Marcus——"

"Eighty thousand pounds!" gasped Margaret and Polly in unison. It was an unheard of amount of money to both of them.

"It is tied up so that no one may touch it but my uncle Marcus, and he may release it when I marry, *if* he approves of my husband. Apparently, he is agreeable to my marrying Cedric, although he has never liked him nor my aunt Serena, either. Oh, how I hoped he would object! But he did not, so it can only mean that he is anxious to be rid of me. I—I—find that very hurtful," she added dolefully.

Margaret was visited by a flash of anger. A mental picture was forming in her mind of an elderly, rich, rather portly gentleman, engrossed, no doubt, in his own comfort, and in his way, fully as selfish and disagreeable as Lady Maulbrais.

"He thinks only of his own pleasures and, I am sure, has not given me a thought since the other day, when he pinched my cheek and wished me happy in my marriage to Cedric!" Annabelle put her head down upon her folded arms and burst into tears. "Oh please, Meg, help me! There's no one else I can turn to, and I would rather die than marry Cedric! Truly! No matter how wicked it is to say such a thing!"

Margaret's face crumpled with distress.

"Please, Annabelle, don't cry so. I shall help you if I can. But nowadays, dear, girls aren't forced into marriages against their will. What on earth can your aunt do to you, after all, if you simply refuse?"

"She can talk!" Annabelle bawled, raising a tear-drenched face. "Do you know what it is like to have someone talking *at* you day and night, about your duty? She says I must marry to save Queen's Keep, to save the Herenford line, and that Mama wanted it that way. And sometimes I become so tired, I think it would be easier to do it than to listen to her anymore. She says I will never get married, for no one wants me but Cedric, and of course she is right about that, too, for I had a season in London and no one did want me. Meg, a whole season, and no one at all proposed to me!" Her voice ended in a wail.

Margaret laughed, but only to herself, for she saw it was deadly serious to Annabelle. What had this lamb expected of her first London season anyway? Buckets of proposals? No doubt she showed to awful disadvantage with that hair and those horrid clothes. Margaret's eyes narrowed. Of course!

That was the reason for the teeth-gnashing combination of colors; the old, old pattern styles, more fitting to a dowager than to a girl of seventeen making her first bow to society. And undoubtedly, everywhere she went, she was in the forbidding company of her aunt? Fortune hunters, who were professional charmers also, could usually find their way to heiresses, no matter how shockingly they may be dressed, if given half a chance. And yesterday she had found Annabelle a charming, even witty, conversationalist, so that one quickly forgot the plain features and insignificant figure; but around her formidable aunt, Annabelle would not show up to such advantage. There were people like Lady Maulbrais who crushed, even paralyzed, one by their presence; and Annabelle, with that pinched little face, sullen, uncommunicative, and without the pretty smile that brought it so sparklingly to life, would be distressingly plain in her aunt's company. Aunt Serena could be sure then that her niece would not "take."

"No one wanted to dance with me," Annabelle sniffled. "At Almack's, only Cedric and some of his horrid friends, whom he brought over and *forced* upon me, asked to stand up with me. Aunt Serena told me not to depend upon Uncle Marcus, for he hated Almack's. It was too stuffy for him, she said, and she was right, for he wasn't there! And Aunt

Serena planned a party, sending out fully a hundred invitations. She said she hoped for no more than a respectable showing in her salons after my poor performance at Almack's. But when Uncle Marcus sent word that he would be out of town and unable to attend——" *Damn the man,* thought Margaret profanely, *couldn't he see how the child had depended upon him?* "I got frightened and started vomiting. I always vomit when I get frightened. I was so sick that Aunt Serena had to call my party off and tell everyone that it was bad fish I ate. But it wasn't bad fish—it was my horrid, n-n-nervous stomach!" She was sobbing again.

Margaret drew her into her arms. At this moment her face was as homely as God had made it, for Annabelle was not a girl who cried prettily, but with red, streaming nose, swollen eyes, and a blotched, patchy face. Her hair was straggling limply across her forehead. But Margaret was both amused and touched by her distress—it seemed so young and unrestrained. It had been years since Margaret herself, with far more cause, had had recourse to tears.

"It seems to me," she said matter-of-factly, dampening a napkin and using a corner of it to wipe Annabelle's streaked face, "that we must get in touch with your uncle Marcus. He will be able to help you and perhaps have some practical remedy to offer. You haven't mentioned—that is, what of his wife? Could she not take you in? If they have young children, she might be grateful for your help——" She was stopped by the odd expression on Annabelle's face.

"He is Marcus Salterson, Meg. He is not married. I—of course you would not know of him, but—my mother left him guardian of my fortune because he is so very rich that he would not covet it as my cousin and aunt do! But Uncle Marcus does not wish to be bothered with me, for he only cares about amusing himself. He was very, very relieved to learn that I was getting married and would be off his hands. I know, because he visited Queen's Keep that day—that day you came. He had not been gone long when you arrived. He was on horseback. You may have even passed him on the road—"

Margaret's eyes widened. The portly old gentleman, fond of his wine and cigars, fled as she readjusted her picture of Annabelle's rich uncle Marcus to one of a lean, dark-haired man astride a wicked-looking black stallion. She remembered how his eyes had raked her mercilessly as she stood in the road, making her tingle with awareness. She had seen him then as being as near like the superb animal he rode as man and beast could be. Each was arrogant and supremely confident of his strength and masculinity. Funny that the man who aroused such intense feelings in her should be the mysterious Marcus Salterson. She had thought she would never see him again. Not that she was likely to now, she reminded herself hastily, if Annabelle was right about his indifference to her.

Of course, he would be a hero to his niece. No wonder the lamb longed for his good opinion! No wonder she was so crushed by his indifference, his failure to attend her party or to stand up with her at Almack's! And how cleverly her aunt had used that indifference to further her own ends! Margaret felt a surge of pure rage. Between them, uncle and aunt, they had mangled the child until it was a wonder she had any strength of will left! And she, for one, had no intention of throwing her back upon their mercy!

"If there is one thing I am determined on, Annabelle, it is that you don't fall into the hands of *either* of your guardians! When they are prepared to forsake their dreadful plan of marrying you to your cousin against your will, then will be the time to think of returning. Meantime, I don't think there is much to choose from between them," Margaret added firmly. "So dry your eyes and let us see what we can do about getting around them."

Later, Annabelle played in the garden with Jodie and the puppy, perfectly carefree now that someone else had taken over her worries, whereas in the kitchen, Margaret braced herself to withstand Polly's disapproval.

"Don't scold me, Polly," she said guiltily.

"Very well, Miss Meg, if you don't wish to hear the truth!" The old woman sniffed worriedly. "But just how do you expect to keep her? I don't like the sound of that uncle or that aunt, and if you don't notify them, they are the sort to be vengeful. Right now, no doubt, the search is quiet because they are trying to keep down scandal, but if she continues to be missing, they'll start to scour the countryside. And bring in the law. Miss Meg, she's going to be found no matter what you do. It may take a while, but sooner or later someone will remember you, and they will trace you to here. And she hasn't much chance of holding out against them if they insist on marrying her to her cousin; so Miss Meg, it would go easier on you if you notified them now."

Margaret merely looked mutinous. Finally Polly sighed resignedly and asked, "How do you expect to hide her until they come for her?"

"I—I'll say she is my little cousin, Susan Plunkett, who is visiting me from someplace far away. So long as she stays out of sight and does not draw attention to herself, it may never be questioned."

"Is she staying out of sight? Is she? Look at her! Chedworth is a village, and you know you can't hide her for long. People will be curious about her. Look at her clothes! You said yourself that they're the finest you've ever seen. How long before someone notices them? And you can't afford to buy her new clothes for a disguise."

Margaret didn't answer, but Polly saw with satisfaction that she was looking thoughtful. When Annabelle came in, leading Jodie by the hand, she broached the suggestion to her.

"I don't want you to tell your uncle where you are," she said quickly. "Merely that you are safe and well, and will be coming home soon. You might mention that you are with a lady of good character who befriended you when you ran away. Such a letter might keep him from putting the Bow Street runners on your trail."

Annabelle saw the wisdom of appeasing her uncle Marcus.

"The other thing is your clothes. They are much too fine for Susan Plunkett, my little cousin from—er—Leeds. I don't have enough money to buy you any new things, and we can't pawn a piece of that jewelry, for it might be traced to you here. If you had just a few shillings—" She paused, embarrassed.

Annabelle, who had been following her words intently, nodded eagerly, her face clearing. "Money? Of course I have money." She jumped up and ran upstairs, then returned with her jewelry box, which she proceeded to empty carelessly on the table. "The money is under the lining of the box."

At first glance, Margaret saw that it was a great deal of money, but she was not prepared for the amount as Annabelle stacked one bill on top of another. "I believe—yes, it is five hundred pounds. Is that enough, Meg?" she asked anxiously.

"Enough?"

"Yes, for the dresses and things."

"My dear, put it away. All but a few pounds. It makes me shiver to think of all that money in my house. We must not let anyone suspect—— Enough, you ask? You can buy all you need with only a few pounds. Do you know, Annabelle, that I maintain this house on no more than a hundred and fifty pounds a year?"

Annabelle was shocked. She had never been encouraged to think of money and had always assumed that every nice, well-bred person, particularly every woman, had it provided for her, in varying degrees, of course. There were, naturally, those women who must earn it, but even here, her picture was blurred by her inexperience. Her governess had come to her from a duke's household after much persuasion on the part of Lady Maulbrais, and she had never allowed her ladyship to forget that the condescension was hers. To know that Margaret, whom she was already regarding as a heroine, managed to keep three people and her neat little cottage on less than Annabelle received quarterly as pin money awed her. She immediately began to ponder how she could help her, which was a new experience for Annabelle, who had never been encouraged to think of anyone but herself.

CHAPTER IV

Marcus Salterson felt a quick surge of irritation as he picked up the envelope from the silver salver beneath his nose and saw that it was from Lady Maulbrais.

"Damn you, Bench, must you awaken me to receive unpleasant news?" He scowled at his valet. "I saw those people only three days ago, and God knows, I have no stomach for another meeting in the near future."

Bench eyed Mr. Salterson sympathetically as he levered himself on his elbow and scratched his bare chest irritably. There was no necessity for his master to tell him when he last saw her ladyship, nor that any communication from her was bound to be unpleasant, since there was not much he did not know about his master's business with his relatives. But he had thought the matter urgent enough, upon speaking personally with the messenger who had brought the letter from Queen's Keep, to justify awakening Mr. Salterson even though he had not come in until past five o'clock this morning, having been, Bench suspected, with that prime bit of fluff whom he had in his keeping (Bench had had the privilege of seeing her with his master at Vauxhall one memorable evening). He knew that his instincts had been right when Mr. Salterson, upon reading the note, was startled into immediate action. Swinging his feet onto the floor and heaving himself out of bed, he called, "Hot water for my shave, Bench, and be quick about it! Where is my dressing gown? I want to see the man who brought this note!"

While Mr. Salterson was out of the room, Bench picked up the discarded letter, but it told him no more than he had already learned from the messenger. Her ladyship was caustic in her brevity.

Annabelle has run away from home. Two days ago. If she is with you, kindly have the decency to notify me. If she is not, advise me, as we have exhausted all avenues here.

The curricle was waiting in the street when Mr. Salterson emerged from his door thirty minutes later, drawing on his riding gloves and wearing a deep scowl on his dark, saturnine face. His grays were fresh, and the groom was having difficulty holding them in check. The curricle was a specially built one for racing, and Bench did not envy the groom who would be forced to hang on to a few strips of wood and metal for the next fifty miles as they drove at Mr. Salterson's usual breakneck speed; but he also knew that Jock would not have traded his treasured position with any man in the kingdom. Mr. Salterson waited with barely concealed impatience while Bench strapped at his feet the portmanteau containing his shaving gear and a few necessities, then nodding curtly to the groom to release the leaders, he took the grays at a spanking pace out of Grosvenor Square and into the London traffic.

There was no delay in showing him into her ladyship's presence when he arrived at Queen's Keep. She was wearing a defiant air that did not speak well for the interview, although she was also extremely pale, as though she had sustained a shock. Lord Maulbrais was with her, also pale and subdued, and when he rose to greet Mr. Salterson, it was without his usual affectations.

"I gather, since you wasted no time in getting here, that the chit is not with you?" Lady Maulbrais gritted through tightly clenched teeth.

With a shock of recognition, Mr. Salterson realized that she was very angry and that her anger was directed toward Annabelle. Ever since reading her note, he had been prey to many conflicting emotions, chief among which was worry; but any anger he felt had been turned upon himself. He knew that he had largely ignored his niece, telling himself relievedly that since she was a girl-child, she might be consigned to Lady Maulbrais's care with an easy conscience; but now he admitted that his reasoning was directed by motives of selfishness.

On the drive to Queen's Keep he had come to several unpalatable conclusions. If the child had gotten into a scandal, or worse, been abducted, he must shoulder the blame of neglect. But anger? No. So far as he could judge from a sketchy observation of them, most of the young girls of Annabelle's age were silly and giddy and prone to imagining themselves in love at all times, and he assumed that Annabelle was no different. After all, she was only seventeen. Undoubtedly, he thought, she had eloped, having been manipulated by some plausible scoundrel who had known that his suit would be rejected out of hand by her guardians. At this point he reminded himself that even this, tragic though it might be, was preferable to abduction or murder. That Lady Maulbrais's chief emotion was anger rather than worry gave Mr. Salterson an unpleasant insight into Annabelle's home life.

"Tell me what you know about this. Everything,

if you please," he commanded crisply, ignoring Lady Maulbrais's vindictive words. "When did you discover that she was gone?"

"Monday morning. She left before daybreak, because she took one of the maid's cloaks that was hanging on a peg in the kitchen passage. Apparently as a disguise," she added bitingly.

"A disguise! Aren't you taking a lot for granted? She might have been abducted for ransom——"

"Hardly," Lady Maulbrais replied dryly. "She left a bolster in her bed, covered over to look as though she was still asleep, in order to delay discovery as long as possible. She also took her portmanteau full of clothes, her mother's jewels, which she had to take from the library safe, and whatever money she may have accumulated from her quarterly allowance."

"Good God! She isn't carrying her jewelry?" Mr. Salterson reacted with horror. "On the high road—unprotected—"

"She is indeed." The dowager's face twisted with fury. "Had I known that she would do such a thing, I would have kept them in my bedroom. But she *stole* them. A fortune in jewelry!" she choked with rage.

"Was there a note?" Mr. Salterson reflected coldly that her ladyship seemed more emotional over the jewelry's disappearance than her niece's.

"No!" The answer was unequivocal.

"I think there must have been," he said sternly. "She would not go away without leaving a note to reassure you. Annabelle would consider that dishonorable."

"How do you know what she considers dishonorable?" she spat at him. "You have never troubled your head to know anything about her."

Lord Cedric shifted his legs and cleared his throat. "Show him the note, Mama," he said apprehensively. "We're going to have to. I never thought Annabelle would go through with the marriage anyway."

"Very well." Lady Maulbrais unclenched her fist slowly and flung the note toward Mr. Salterson. "Make what you will of it."

Mr. Salterson went over to the long windows opening onto the park, and turning his back to the room, read the note. He found it childishly appealing and felt an unaccustomed tightness in his throat.

Dear Aunt Serena, Annabelle had written in her careful, schoolgirl hand, *I am running away. Please forgive me, but I must. I am sorry not to do as you ask, but believe me, Aunt Serena, I cannot marry Cedric no matter what Mama wished. I am sorry to displease you, Aunt, but do please understand and do not make me come home and marry Cedric.*

Mr. Salterson's face twisted. He stayed where he was, tapping the note against his thumbnail. "It seems, madam, that you have been applying pressure to your niece, and I have been a party to it by my silence. When we get her back——" He stopped, "Who is the man? Do you know?"

"There is no man!" Lady Serena was affronted. "Don't be vulgar, Salterson. If you mean that you think she had help in getting away, I am inclined to agree with you. Otherwise, Cedric would have found some trace of her, and God knows, he has scoured the countryside these past two days. I interviewed the servants as discreetly as possible, of course, but learned nothing from them. However, you may have better luck. You might start with Pendleton, Annabelle's abigail. She knows the whole story, for it was she who first discovered Annabelle was missing. She came to Queen's Keep with Amelia before Annabelle was born and is absolutely loyal to her. She has never liked me and has stubbornly refused to say a word whenever I question her. You may be able to get her to tell you something since, logically, she would be the only person in whom Annabelle would have confided."

Pendleton was an elderly woman whom Mr. Salterson remembered slightly from the days when his sister lived at home. She entered the salon with a truculent expression which changed to a grudging smile when she saw him.

"Don't blame Miss Annabelle, sir. My poor lamb was desperate about this marriage."

"Hold your tongue, Pendleton!" snapped Lady

Maulbrais angrily. "Mr. Salterson is not interested in your opinion, merely in whatever information you can give him about Miss Annabelle's whereabouts. Did she say anything at all to give you a hint of what she was planning to do?"

Had Mr. Salterson not been so worried, he would have laughed at the look of rigid dislike with which Pendleton regarded her ladyship before turnng away pointedly to look at him.

"It's important, Pendleton," he said gently. "Can you tell me anything that might give me a clue to finding Miss Annabelle? Could anyone have helped her get away?"

"I have been thinking about that, sir, and I have wondered if it could have been that lady. She talked to her, sir, I know that. But could Miss Annabelle have persuaded her to take her up?"

"What lady?" he asked quickly.

"She sheltered here from the rain. A nice, pretty lady with the prettiest, friendliest little smile——"

Lady Maulbrais gave a hiss. "That creature! She appeared out of nowhere asking for shelter, and I allowed her to remain while her carriage wheel was being repaired. I could hardly do less, although what was such a creature doing on the roadside alone without even a woman to accompany her? She only stayed a short time, then her coachman returned for her. But Annabelle could not have—— It was the day before that the woman was here!"

Pendleton sniffed and looked at Mr. Salterson. "Miss Annabelle overheard her ladyship and felt sorry for the young lady. She was put in a back parlor without a fire or hot tea, and her a lady and dripping wet at that. My little lady carried her a tray with her own hands, for she knew the servants were afeared to disobey her ladyship. She stayed quite a while, talking to her. Of course, I know she didn't leave with her then! But perhaps something was said—— I mean Miss Annabelle liked her, and she came back to her room laughing, telling me that the lady took her for a governess or a lady's companion or something."

Mr. Salterson remembered very well the dazzling young woman in the yellow carriage whom he had directed to Queen's Keep for shelter and who had apparently been given it grudgingly. She would not have deliberately lured Annabelle away, he thought, but perhaps she dropped some innocent remark, as Pendleton suspected, that might indicate in which direction Annabelle would have gone. Certainly, it was worth looking into, particularly as there seemed to be nothing else to guide them.

"Do you know this young woman's name? Or her home?"

"No, sir. Only that she was to spend the night at the inn and was to leave the following morning. She told Miss Annabelle that much."

"Good. They may know something there." He turned to the dowager. "Madam, I am taking my leave of you and will notify you as soon as I find your niece. However, at the same time I am serving notice on you that I will assume her future guardianship."

"I am sure you are welcome to it," Lady Maulbrais snapped contemptuously. "And her reputation, too, if it still exists after this escapade. My Cedric would not have her now under any circumstances."

"Quite." Mr. Salterson agreed with rigid politeness. He turned to Pendleton. "Pack yours and your mistress's things. I will send for you as soon as I return to London. As for you, madam, I suggest you keep your tongue between your teeth about this affair, and instruct your son and the servants to do the same. If I find that Annabelle's reputation has suffered on account of anything that has come from this place, I will know to whom to apply for satisfaction." He looked at Cedric meaningfully.

"Oh, I say, sir!" Cedric surged to his feet, stammering incoherently. "Don't—please don't—we wouldn't—that is, never should have proposed the marriage, as I told Mama all the time. I knew it wouldn't suit. Tried to tell her but—— Please, Mr. Salterson, don't tax yourself with any worry that any of us would ever—my cousin, after all, and a

Herenford and under my protection, and we would be the last people in the world to——"

"Not any longer," Mr. Salterson said briefly. "Under your protection, that is. But I will accept your assurances, Lord Maulbrais. From now on you may look to me to care for my niece's good name."

"I wish you well of her," Lady Maulbrais said viciously, "for she will be on your hands so long as you live unless you can persuade some fool to overlook her deficiencies for her future."

"Ah. You did, didn't you, madam?" he asked smoothly.

She flushed. "You are removing her illegally, you know. Rightfully, you still must discharge her accrued indebtedness, but I presume that no matter how much I insist you will still ignore your obligations?"

Mr. Salterson nodded. "You are correct, madam. I will. Your share in Annabelle's fortune is at an end unless, of course," he added ironically, "you can persuade her to come to your relief." With that cutting blow, he bowed himself out.

Personally, he had no faith that Annabelle might be with the young woman whom he had seen, but she was the only lead he had, and obviously something had put a spur to the child to make her take such a drastic step. Could it have been the young woman plus his own visit to the Keep that same afternoon? With an aching compunction, he remembered the woebegone little figure following him outside as he mounted his horse. He suspected that she had been trying to summon the courage to ask for his help. And he had ruffled her hair and talked of bridal presents! Could she have then turned in desperation to the young woman in the yellow carriage, even—asked for her help?

He found out the answer almost at once. At the inn he easily learned the identity of the owner of the yellow carriage, for the coachman had talked freely to the stable hands, in the manner of his kind. He did not learn, unfortunately, the name or destination of the passenger.

"Did she by any chance add another passenger? Not that night, but the following morning?"

"Kitchen maid said she did," was the indifferent reply. "She saw 'un pick up a lass at the crossroad."

The kitchen maid was unavailable for questioning, but Mr. Salterson felt that he had been given enough positive information to justify a hasty visit the following morning to Lawton Grange, where he had been told the coachman and carriage hailed from. He cursed again, as he had been doing all day, Lady Maulbrais's dilatoriness in sending for him, which added to the difficulty in following a cold trail. He was almost compelled, now, to backtrack to the carriage's point of origin rather than forge ahead, as he longed to do.

Lawton Grange was a fine estate located on the

Wells Road a few miles out of Bath. It had extensive grounds enclosed by a heavy fence, and a pair of forbidding iron gates manned by a gatekeeper. He directed Mr. Salterson up a gravel carriage drive, which he said swept past the house to the stables.

"Make sure none of the patients try to take your horses," he called after him. "Look for the stable boy!"

Mr. Salterson was still puzzling over that remark as he wended his way through a parklike woods and out onto a wide, clipped lawn, where a number of persons were strolling about, always in pairs. The truth began to dawn upon him, but he inquired of the stable boy.

"Oh yes, sir." The boy was astonished at his ignorance. "Everyone hereabouts knows about Dr. Stockton. This is his home, and he turned it into a hospital for patients." He coughed significantly and tapped his head. "We don't have any trouble with them, sir, for they're not violent. Just gentle and quiet-like, and sometimes a little wishful of going home. That's why we must guard the horses and the gates."

Mr. Salterson was somewhat relieved to learn that he would be interviewing a doctor, whom he expected to make short work of. But in Dr. Stockton he came up against a will as inflexible as his own. He was received by the doctor in his study, offered a fine Madeira wine, and then taking up his card and studying the name, Dr. Stockton said, with a humorous little twist of his mouth, "You might as well unburden yourself, Mr. Salterson. I have been watching you try to make up your mind about me. Have you decided that I, a repository of secrets, am responsible enough to hear yours, also?"

Mr. Salterson hastily revised his original story. This pleasant-faced gentleman with the wise, humorous eyes could be depended upon to keep his own counsel. So, modifying the truth slightly to place Annabelle's age downward to about twelve, he laid his cards on the table. Dr. Stockton was sympathetic, but said positively that the lady in question would not have been so remiss as to spirit off a runaway child.

"Then she is not Mrs. Stockton?" Mr. Salterson asked bluntly, conscious, for some obscure reason, of a strong feeling of relief.

"No." Dr. Stockton smiled ruefully. She was not, although he hoped someday—— Here, he stopped self-consciously. She was a widow, a Mrs. Robert Terrell, who was visiting a patient in his hospital. To imagine that a gentlewoman such as Mrs. Terrell would lend herself to an abduction was an absurdity, he added.

Mr. Salterson, who by this time was merely on the track of an address, informed Dr. Stockton that she *had* lent herself to the abduction, for his niece had been seen getting into her carriage. Now, if he could have her direction, he would leave the good doctor to his work and be on his way.

Dr. Stockton, shaken, rallied and answered with slightly more heat that he had no intention of giving Mrs. Terrell's address to *anyone* without her permission.

"You know that I can get it, don't you?" Mr. Salterson, thoroughly ruffled by this time, snapped. "If I put the affair into the hands of the Bow Street runners, your Mrs. Terrell may find herself facing a criminal charge—"

"*If* she is guilty of wrongdoing." Dr. Stockton made a steeple of his fingers and glared at Mr. Salterson over them. "And why, may I ask, haven't you already called in the Bow Street runners, sir?" His eyes narrowed. "Could it be that this is not a child after all and you suspect a runaway elopement? I think that you have not been entirely frank with me, sir. No. I will write to Mrs. Terrell and ask her if she wishes to see you—"

"Never mind," Mr. Salterson said disagreeably. "I'll see to it without your help. It will be an easy matter to get the information from Lord Buckhaven." It was a shot in the dark, and he was surprised to see how it hit its mark.

Dr. Stockton jerked his head up and cried indignantly. "Oh yes, I am sure you may! It will be an easy matter, indeed, if he thinks he can learn something to Mrs. Terrell's discredit. But you shall not, I tell you, get anything further from *me!*"

Since he had already learned what he wished to know, Mr. Salterson took his leave of Dr. Stockton, who was by now extremely hostile. He had indeed been probing when he mentioned Lord Buckhaven, but obviously Mrs. Terrell was a connection of his and equally disliked. Not that Mr. Salterson put much store in that, for Lord Buckhaven's enemies were numerous.

Lord Buckhaven's family was not altogether unknown to Mr. Salterson, although he was not familiar with its individual members. He knew the old lord, of course, as a thoroughly disagreeable old man who had the reputation of unleashing frightening bursts of temper when provoked. His heir, too, was not well liked, although his sin seemed to be one of sullen moodiness. Mr. Salterson had known Giles Terrell when they were both at Oxford and had thought him a thoroughly good fellow. He had only been nineteen and showing a scholarly bent when he was yanked out of school and summarily married off to a woman at least ten years his senior, who was reputed to be quite an heiress. She had presented him in due course with a female child, and it was bruited about that they now lived apart. Mr. Salterson recalled another rumor, equally vague, that Giles was Lord Buckhaven's only surviving son, his younger brothers having died in violent accidents. He wondered if the beautiful young woman whom he had met on the road was the widow of one of Giles's brothers.

Mr. Salterson arrived home by late afternoon, dead tired. He would have given twenty golden guineas if he could have sought the comfort of his study, put his feet up, and enjoyed a glass of port while dwelling pleasurably on the prospect of a visit that night to the lady who lived under his protection. However, he shrugged off the temptation to give way to so much as a few hours of self-indulgence. He was haunted by anxiety for Annabelle and conscious of a strong feeling of urgency. Therefore, calling for Bench, he ordered a bath, a shave, and for his evening clothes to be set out.

Mr. Salterson could, when he so desired, dress extremely well. His usual careless style was a result of indifference and a matter of personal anguish to his valet. Impeccably tailored by the finest craftsmen, his coats were cut to set upon the tall, muscular figure as though they were molded there. He had no need of wadding nor buckram to disguise narrow shoulders or spindly calves. With a fabulous collection of family jewelry from which to choose what he liked, he never wore anything but a single, flawless emerald on his ring finger, not even diamond studs on his shirtfront. Tonight was no exception, but when Bench pronounced himself satisfied, he thought his master would do very well.

"He's not visiting his lightskirt tonight," he mused to himself. He was standing at a salon window, watching Mr. Salterson hail a chairman. "In the first place, he told me he'd be back early, and second, he didn't carry a geegaw, like he usually does when he's been away from her for a day or two. No, he has something else on his mind."

"Faro?" suggested one of the very junior footmen, who was standing behind him.

"Faro?" Bench managed to sound both snubbing and lofty at the same time. "No, not faro, my man, for he'd never be worrying if it was just cards. When you have known your master as long as *I* have, you'll know he's no gamester." The young upstart needed a setdown, thought Bench. He had the advantage of knowing about Miss Annabelle so he could guess his master was on business connected with her, but he had no intention of sharing *that* information with his inferiors.

Bench would have been even more astonished if he could have followed Mr. Salterson, whose wandering seemed to be aimless. First he called in at Brooke's, where he was hailed by acquaintances and persuaded to loiter for a few minutes. Not finding what he sought, however, he stopped in at a private gaming house on Mount Street, but soon left. Next he proceeded to White's, where the play was deep. There he found the prey he sought.

Giles Terrell had apparently just left the table, for he was standing alone, a deep scowl on his face, watching the players. He looked up in surprise when he was accosted by Mr. Salterson, who spoke genially to him.

"Good evening, Giles. I wish for a private conversation with you." Giles obediently withdrew to an anteroom that was, for the moment, empty. "I would like to know how I might find Mrs. Robert Terrell. Does she reside in this city or somewhere else?"

Giles blinked. "What d'you want with her?" he asked in a surly voice.

"Surely that's between the two of us, isn't it?" Mr. Salterson asked smoothly.

"Not if you wish her direction from me, it ain't. I don't go around giving out such facts about my brother's widow unless I know why."

Mr. Salterson was relieved to learn that he had guessed right. A vague impression of a rumor—something scandalous—tugged at his memory, something unsavory about Robert Terrell, wasn't it? He eyed Giles measuringly.

"I have a small legal action against her. I need the direction for the bailiff."

Giles Terrell shrugged. "Then it's m'father you want, not me." He sounded absolutely indifferent.

"He hates the chit. I have nothing against her and see no reason why I should aid you in putting the bailiffs on her trail."

Mr. Salterson changed his tactics. "I can find out from him, of course. However, I'll admit that—er—I bent the truth a little for reasons of delicacy. I have a gold bracelet that belongs to her. She dropped it accidentally during an encounter we had, and I wish to return it to her."

Giles Terrell gave a guffaw of laughter. "That's more like it! Want to offer her a carte blanche, eh? Can't blame you. She's a beautiful woman."

"What makes you think your sister-in-law has joined the muslin society, Terrell?" Mr. Salterson asked icily.

"Lud, man, what else can she do? She's a pauper. The old man will never allow her to contract a respectable marriage, not if he can put a spoke in the wheel. She has two or three dependents to support, so what else can she do? I wish her nothing but luck; if she can acquire you for a protector, she'll be set up for life, and the old man will be left gnashing his teeth. That would suit me just fine! As I said, m'father is the one who'd like to see her assigned to perdition. Oh, I'll gladly give you her direction. You'll find her at Mulberry Cottage, in Chedworth."

"You honor me." Mr. Salterson bowed coldly and strolled leisurely out of the club.

CHAPTER V

Having taken Annabelle's troubles onto her own
shoulders, so to speak, Margaret decided defiantly
that if the child was going to be forced into an
odious marriage with a cousin she detested, then
she would at least have something to remember
that was pleasant. She intended to crowd as much
fun into the remaining time that was left before
Annabelle was returned to her prison as the village
of Chedworth could supply. Not one party, not one
picnic nor ball nor berry-picking was going to be
passed up if it was in her power to see that Annabelle went. She knew that the story of Susan
Plunkett could be sustained only so long as it was
not questioned too closely, but so far as the inhabi-

tants of Chedworth were concerned, it would not occur to any of them to do so.

It would be a simple story, in fact, the simpler the better: a little cousin of her mother's, who had come from Leeds to visit Margaret for a while, with her background purposely left vague. Annabelle took to the story enthusiastically—so much so that she had to be restrained from embellishing upon it.

Annabelle's reasoning was simple. She had made her confession, placed her trust in Margaret's ability to rescue her, and thereupon, she proceeded to forget about it. There were times, of course, like the first day, when Polly thought it a good idea for the good of Annabelle's soul to remind her of just what she owed to Margaret. Then, Annabelle felt guilty and subdued to think that she had recklessly embroiled her friend in a scrape that might have embarrassing consequences. But on the whole, since not even Polly had the heart to suggest to her that she had also placed her friend in jeopardy of prison, Annabelle found it easy to forget all about Queen's Keep. She was of a sunny disposition normally, so was thoroughly happy, finding only praise and envy for Margaret's life in the little cottage and taking to village life as though she had a talent for it. It reminded her of the more pleasant aspects of Queen's Keep, when as a child, she had been left alone for weeks at a time in the care of Pendleton, her nurse, while her aunt did the

London season. She had been free to spend as much time as she liked in the kitchen, listening to the housemaids gossip. That was before her governess had come, a forbidding woman whose personality precisely fit Lady Maulbrais's idea of a perfect companion for the niece she was grooming as her successor.

When told to write her uncle Marcus, Annabelle had forgotten Margaret's warning "the simpler the better," and allowed herself to get carried away. She embroidered upon her story of a lady who had rescued her, putting it all down upon paper without any idea that her uncle would have no difficulty in reading between the lines.

The first morning, having sustained a scolding from Polly, Annabelle's little woebegone face pricked Margaret's conscience until she was led to suggest that they make a trip to the village, where she hoped the diversion of visiting the dressmaker might do something for Annabelle's lowered spirits. She was glad to see Gussie Nettlefield and Lizzie Stedbelow, apparently upon errands for their mothers. They were two young ladies who were Annabelle's age, and their frisky spirits might prove to be just the thing needed to turn the girl's mind away from her own troubles. She introduced the girls to her little "cousin," and it did not take five minutes before they were chattering as if they were old friends, with Annabelle holding her own very well. Margaret listened indulgently for a while, then felt reassured enough to leave them while she searched among the bolts of fabrics for the ones that were suitable for a very young lady.

There had been no question about the need for additional clothes. A closer examination of Annabelle's portmanteau had shown Margaret, as nothing else could, that she had packed it herself, probably for the first time in her life, and without any notion of what she would need for a runaway trip to the country or even one to the city. She had stuffed in as many as two ball dresses and several lesser-party dresses, but she had nothing that remotely approached what she would need in a country village except for the little muslin that she was wearing when she ran away. She had remembered lingerie and white gloves and even a lace fan with ivory sticks, but she had forgotten such necessaries as a nightgown, stockings, slippers, comb, brush, tooth powder, a bonnet, and a dozen other items that Margaret would have counted as essential to one's toilet. Annabelle's most pressing need was for simple garments. From the way the girls were chattering of Assemblies and balls, Margaret could see an evening party or two in the future, but she thought that a buttercup-yellow crepe among Annabelle's things would do very well, once it was stripped of its elaborate trim and a simple knot or two of ribbons were substituted. Margaret had been sighing wistfully over an emerald-green satin for herself, but she put it resolutely away and concentrated on suitable things for a very young lady. A walking dress could be fashioned from this fine cambric of a deep, rich blue, and a pretty French muslin printed with rosebuds would do for afternoon calls. And while she was about it, she thought recklessly, why not buy this length of green voile, which would be an obvious choice for a morning dress?

The girls left the dressmaker's shop and wandered outside while she went on to conclude the business that had been all-absorbing to Annabelle until now. Margaret had with her the garish pink gown which Lady Maulbrais had chosen for her niece to wear to the ball that had been postponed.

"I'll have to pick it to pieces, Miss Meg." Mrs. Tompkins peered at it shortsightedly. "It looks so rich. And so heavy! And no wonder, for it's encrusted with pearls. It was made by a London dressmaker, wasn't it? I have never seen stitching like this."

"I don't care what you do with it," Margaret said impatiently. "I only brought it along for the measurements. I certainly don't think it would do for a young girl, do you?"

"Oh, no," the dressmaker said decidedly. "It was made for an older woman. Not only the material, but the trim tells me that. But it seems almost—too beautiful to pick apart."

"Nonsense!" said Margaret heartily, but she was thoughtful. She was certain now that Serena Maulbrais had chosen her ward's clothes with a purpose.

In the meantime, Annabelle had broadened her horizon to include a fair, very tall young man named George Mendenhall. George, passing on horseback with no more than a slight tilt of his hat, had paused, attracted by an unfamiliar blond head among the two dark ones. Introductions were quickly made, and George found himself thoroughly intrigued by Mrs. Terrell's little cousin. Not pretty, no, but a taking little thing when animated, he thought. As for Annabelle, she was conscious of looking her best. Margaret had dressed her hair in a smooth fashion that was an improvement over corkscrew curls, and she was flushed with success over the flirtation that she had set up with this young giant. He, in turn, was charmed with demureness and fluttering eyelashes.

"I must say, Miss Susan, your cousin said nothing about a visitor. Why didn't she warn us to expect you?"

"Measles." Annabelle dimpled and lowered her eyes. "All of my brothers and sisters have come down with it, and I was the nurse. My mama felt that I was due a rest."

"Measles?" George was taken aback.

"I have had them," Annabelle reassured him. "But I was so tired with staying up day and night, nursing them all——"

"I should say so!" George replied feelingly. "How many——"

"Six. A round half-dozen. Three of each. And I am the eldest. There is Clarissa and Timothy and Elizabeth Ann——"

A firm clasp on her elbow stopped her fantasy in full flight. "Susan, my dear. I am sure we must be getting home."

"Ma'am, may I—we—call on you this afternoon? My mother is planning a small evening party, and my brother wishes to invite you to it himself. And of course, Miss Plunkett. Er—please, ma'am, do not tell Lucian that I have spoken out of turn, for he expressly told me to wait until he——" George stopped confusedly.

Margaret smiled. "Of course you may call if you wish, George. And I shan't say anything. We will be home after three o'clock."

As they were walking away, Margaret said sternly, "My dear Annabelle, had you not better control your imagination? The last story, for instance, could get you into serious trouble. What if the next time you were called upon to name the six brothers and sisters you forgot them? Think of your consternation if George or one of the girls had to remind you of Elizabeth Ann?"

"I did not think of that." Annabelle hung her head guiltily.

"Bear it in mind and keep the stories of your past as simple as possible," Margaret said crisply. They were stepping across the street, and their way was suddenly barred by a trap that pulled directly into their path. Harnessed to it was a fat, dappled pony. The woman handling the reins smiled archly at them.

She was very beautiful, with glossy black hair, white, camellia-soft skin, and reddened lips. The figure that was molded into her blue riding habit, which was resplendent with gold buttons across her generous bosom, was rather statuesque and was shown off to a nicety by the costume. A high Wellington hat with a dashing feather completed the ensemble, and Annabelle, blinking at the splendor, wondered why she was in Chedworth when she was more suited to a London park.

Margaret introduced her to Annabelle as Irene Marshbanks, in a colorless voice that indicated a notable lack of enthusiasm.

"I thought I knew all my cousin Margaret's relatives, but until now I have never heard of you. Are you from a big family, my dear?" she asked.

"Susan has a family," Margaret said repressively.

"We all have families," Irene replied smoothly. "I meant a *large* family. Not like—Jodie's. Did you know that little Jodie is my cousin, Susan?" she added smilingly.

Something was amiss. Margaret was holding Annabelle's arm rigidly, but at Irene's innocently expressed question she stiffened slightly. Annabelle was not usually quick to catch subtleties, but she could see that the reference to Jodie had some distressing significance for Margaret. It occurred to her that Irene Marshbanks had just planted a poison dart of malice into Margaret's quivering flesh.

"Shall I see you at the Mendenhall evening party?" Irene added.

"We have not yet been formally invited," Margaret replied.

"Lud, neither have I! But the county is too woefully thin of eligible persons at this time of the year for either of us to be slighted. I have already ordered the green satin I particularly desired on the strength of receiving an invitation, and so I shall tell Lucian Mendenhall if he dares to forget me! By the way, Margaret dear, I do hope you will wear that lovely blue of yours again. You look so—nice—in it!" Margaret trembled. Another dart had found its mark, one that Annabelle herself could not miss this time.

"Speaking of clothes, child," Irene added affably,

turning to Annabelle. "Where did you get that beautiful thing I saw Mrs. Tompkins pulling to pieces? It is London made, I swear. Not your style, of course, but positively the most gorgeous thing I have seen since my last London ball."

"Oh Lud, ma'am, now you know my secret." Annabelle tittered in an astonishingly silly manner that jerked Margaret's head around in amazement. "There are seven of us, just as you guessed. A large family indeed! When my lady sent her ball dress from the castle to my mama and asked her to find a use for it, Mama could not refuse, now could she? Not when it was my lady who gave it to us, intending for one of the girls to wear it to county parties! But it was unsuitable, Mama saw that at once. *She* did not want it, nor did we, so Mama thought it might do as a dressmaking model for me. La, how pleased she will be to know it was useful to someone! Why, ma'am, since you like it so, I will be glad for you to have it as soon as the dressmaker has finished with it!" she added artlessly.

A deep, unbecoming flush covered Irene's offended face. She was struck speechless, then with a stifled cluck to her pony she drove off abruptly, leaving the girls standing in the street.

"Is that disagreeable woman really your cousin, Meg?" Annabelle asked briskly, not noticing the expression of awe on Margaret's face as she looked at her.

"She was my husband's cousin," Margaret explained carefully. Her face was pink, as though she were suppressing laughter with difficulty. "She was married to Oliver Marshbanks of Netherwood. He was a gentleman much older, and when he died, she sold Netherwood to Lucian Mendenhall because she said it was too large for her to maintain. It was—er—assumed by most of us that she would leave Chedworth, since she had often said how bored she was here and how much she adored London, but to our surprise, she chose to stay on. She bought a smaller cottage called Willow Lodge."

"Is Mr. Mendenhall a bachelor?" Annabelle asked shrewdly.

"Why yes, as a matter of fact, he is," Margaret replied gently.

"An eligible bachelor? Handsome? With a nice fortune?"

"It is said that he has ten thousand a year," Margaret replied. A dimple quivered in the corner of her mouth.

"Meg, you know!" Annabelle crowed. "That's why she has stayed on here!"

"It is rumored in the village that that might be the explanation, but it is gossip," Margaret replied reprovingly. "Mr. Mendenhall is a very pleasant gentleman who has shown himself to be perfectly capable of taking evasive action." Her eyes danced. "Perhaps he learned his—er—maneuvers from the

Iron Duke, under whom he served. At any rate, he is much too busy looking after his stepmother and half brother and sister to allow himself to become involved with Mrs. Marshbanks's tactics. Mrs. Mendenhall was very depressed after her husband's death, and it was thought that she might benefit from a change of scenery. That is why Mr. Mendenhall bought Netherwood and moved from Yorkshire."

"And the party, Meg? Are we going to attend the party?" Annabelle asked eagerly.

A shadow passed over Margaret's face, but she answered in a determinedly cheerful voice. "Indeed, we shall! We must think about clothes. Let me see, I think your jonquil crepe will be just the thing if I can remake it in time. It merely needs a few alterations to make it quite suitable."

Annabelle came to a dead halt. She remembered Irene's malicious reference to the blue dress, her boastful remark about the green satin, and then Margaret's wistful face as she fingered the same green satin.

"I—I forgot something. I have to go back."

Margaret stopped too. "But you can't." She was dismayed. "George and Lucian—Mr. Mendenhall—will be there in a few minutes and——"

But Annabelle explained rapidly that she had suddenly changed her mind about the coal-scuttle bonnet ornamented with waving ostrich plumes.

."I don't think it's your type!" Margaret called after the flying figure, suppressing a shudder at the vision of Annabelle in an inverted coal scuttle.

"Then something else will be!" Annabelle flung over her shoulder.

Annabelle was not blind to Margaret's poverty, for in spite of an upbringing that was designed to make her arrogant and uncaring, she had a great deal of shrewdness and generosity of spirit. She had already learned from Polly that Margaret's life had changed drastically after her marriage and Teresa's illness, and she knew that she was living on a pittance and Sir Humphrey Stedbelow's charity. Polly had told her that he allowed them to live in Mulberry Cottage, although he could ill afford the loss of the rent himself. Annabelle's eyes were opened to the fact that the dress that Margaret wore to the village had had its hem turned twice, and her three-year-old bonnet was destined for another season. Polly's motive was simple: she intended for Annabelle to know what it meant to Margaret to befriend her. Annabelle did, and her anger, quick to rise, was on a steady boil: she did not intend for Irene Marshbanks to attend the Netherwood party in a dress that was meant to shame Margaret.

She ran all the way without stopping and found little Mrs. Tompkins perfectly willing to cooperate in her scheme to surprise Margaret with a green-satin party dress.

"I don't care how you make it up for her so long as it is stunning!" she said rashly. "But it *must* outdo Mrs. Marshbanks's dress! It must overshadow hers! I want her wild with envy!"

Mrs. Tomkins's face flushed excitedly. She had been taken into little Miss Plunkett's confidence, and it had been an exciting experience. She always had been fond of Margaret Terrell and had found no pleasure in her reversed fortunes. But more particularly, no one as vulnerable to Mrs. Marshbanks's slights and snubs as her dressmaker could fail to be titillated by the opportunity to best her.

"I wish I had the time to really do it justice," she said regretfully. "Then I could sew on the seed pearls from your gown, my dear. But I must finish Mrs. Marshbanks's dress first and——"

"Hire more people," Annabelle said promptly, pulling a wad of pound notes out of her reticule. "As many as it takes!"

When she returned to Mulberry Cottage, she found their guests had already arrived, and Margaret was impatiently waiting for her. A quick look reassured her that Annabelle was not carrying a hatbox, so she relaxed and introduced her to George's half brother, Lucian. Large and fair also, he had the commanding presence and assurance of a man who has seen much of the world. He was very anxious for them to come to the evening party his stepmother was giving, and from the hesitant way he broached the subject, he apparently felt that there was some doubt about it.

"I hope that Miss Susan will be my advocate," he said smilingly. "Frankly, Miss Susan, I am glad that you are here. Your cousin is too prone to turn down our invitations. With you here, she cannot deny us the pleasure of her company any longer. I hope that you will see to it that she accompanies you everywhere, Miss Susan. In fact, I have brought over an invitation from my stepmother for both of you to return with my brother and me to Netherwood. She wishes to meet Miss Susan, but she is particularly anxious for your advice, Miss Meg, on what she should serve at her party."

Annabelle thought demurely that Lucian's request showed a touch of genius. There was no better way to make sure of Margaret than to request her help. For the first time, her eyes were opened to the possibility of Lucian as a suitor. The signs certainly pointed in that direction, and it might explain Irene's jealous spite.

As for Mrs. Mendenhall, the eager way she greeted Margaret when they arrived showed that she was anxious to ask her help. Sitting with her was her daughter, Chloe, a pretty girl of about fifteen who was obviously delighted to see someone of Annabelle's age. Presently, after having consumed most of the food on the tea tray, George grew restless and suggested that his sister and Annabelle accompany him to the stables to see the horses.

"Lucian intends to ask Mrs. Terrell to allow you to ride tomorrow," George explained. "Naturally, he will expect her to join you. Er—I hope you can ride?" he added doubtfully.

"Of course I can ride," Annabelle said loftily. "But must you take me out of the room before he asks her?"

"He expects her to object," George explained. "He will be offering his horses, and Miss Meg never likes to be under obligation to anyone. He is depending upon Mama to tip the scales for him, and he did not want us in the room when he asks her. You see, Miss Meg used to be a notable horsewoman; her father's hunters were known throughout the shire. But she had to give them up when he died, and it is the one thing she misses more than any other. Lucian was told that by the vicar. He is hoping to persuade her by pointing out that it will bring you pleasure. Mama will add her voice to his, to bring her around. Silly Susan!" he added when Annabelle looked blank. "Can't you see that my brother is head over heels in love with Miss Meg?"

"I thought he might be," Annabelle replied, "but I don't understand why he chooses such an elaborate method to show her. Why doesn't he simply ask her to marry him?"

Chloe giggled, and George looked patient. "He has. Several times. But she always refuses. Anyone less in love would have given up, but not Lucian. He says he will never give her up so long as she doesn't marry anyone else. He is patiently waiting for her to recover from her husband's death."

"Do you mean—she is still in mourning? After all these years? How—foolish!"

"I agree. Miss Meg is very true to her first love."

"Oh, it's not fair," Annabelle said impetuously. "He would be perfect for her! And she is so good, so—so sweet! She deserves someone nice! I hope he won't grow tired of waiting for her!"

"Never! Oh, Irene Marshbanks would give anything for him to propose to *her*, but Lucian never would!"

"Mama is petrified for fear he will," Chloe remarked. "She says that Netherwood is not big enough to hold both of them."

"Oh, that would be frightful!" Annabelle said thoughtfully, her brain in a whirl with schemes.

It would solve all of Meg's problems to have a rich husband like Lucian, she thought, and moreover, prevent George from having a disagreeable sister-in-law like Irene. She did not know how she could help, but she could not allow such a terrible thing to happen to George, who was rapidly becoming her very best friend.

CHAPTER VI

During the next few days, Annabelle made the heady discovery that it was easy to become popular in a small village. One did not need beauty; one merely had to be a new face, keep one's head, and avoid making a social blunder. Chedworth, tame by London standards, was delightful and absorbing to one who had never been allowed to even walk about the grounds of Queen's Keep without the companionship of a maid or a governess. Mulberry Cottage itself was a sheer joy, as well kept outside as in. It presented a pleasing picture with its thatched roof and a wisteria vine shading the front entrance. Neatly trimmed shrubbery and flower beds decorated the front with a brushed pathway leading to the gate. In back was a small, well-tended vegetable garden, with fruit trees espaliered to a lattice dividing the garden from the poultry enclosure. Altogether, every inch had been put to use in a thrifty, well-managed way, and if Annabelle had been granted a boon, she would have wished for nothing more than to stay at Mulberry Cottage forever.

Besides the horseback rides, furnished through the courtesy of Lucian Mendenhall, there was a dinner party at the home of Gussie Nettlefield. It was a rambling old house, filled to the overflowing with numerous Nettlefield children. To this, Margaret wore her faithful "blue" and Annabelle her muslin. She found Gussie's parents frankly vulgar. He was in trade, and Mrs. Nettlefield, increasing with her eleventh, wore a ruffled "wrapper." In London they would not have been allowed past the butler, for her aunt had always warned her that the vulgar became dreadfully encroaching if they were encouraged, but Annabelle could not believe the kindly Nettlefields would ever encroach. So far as vulgarity went, that too was relative. Mr. Nettlefield's behavior was no different from the Prince Regent's, and Mrs. Nettlefield reminded her of a certain duchess who was a close friend of her aunt's.

Mrs. Marshbanks was not present at the Nettlefield's, but she was invited to a picnic given by Sir

Humphrey and Lady Elizabeth Stedbelow on the lawn of Oakenfield. To this, Margaret wore a faded French muslin, but George and Annabelle were gratified to note that Lucian could not keep his eyes off her.

Annabelle was also glad to see that Lucian was a determined suitor. Using Annabelle as his excuse, he had the Mendenhall carriage at their door every day, carrying an invitation to tea or a ride or any other outing that might occur to him.

Therefore, the green satin dress became a matter of first importance to Annabelle. She made frequent trips to the village to check upon its progress, and when the day of the party finally arrived and she made her last visit to pick it up, she saw that it was everything she had hoped for. It was simple yet elegant, and fully as gorgeous as a London import, with the addition of the seed pearls which Mrs. Tomkins's henchwoman had spent hours sewing to the fabric. Mrs. Tomkins packed it carefully in a box and Annabelle carried it home where, with Polly's help, she managed to keep it hidden until Margaret came upstairs to dress. Seeing it upon the bed in all its splendor, Margaret burst into tears and threw her arms around Annabelle. Polly beamed as she watched them, her antagonism momentarily forgotten.

A loud rap at the front door interrupted them as they were dressing.

"Bother!" Annabelle ran to the mirror and began to ruthlessly tug at her hair with the brush. "They're early and I'm not near ready!"

"It can't be the Mendenhall carriage this early," Margaret said, frowning slightly as the door closed behind Polly. "Lucian said seven o'clock." She went to the window, and saw a smart curricle drawn up to the gate. "No, it's someone else. Could it be George?"

After a short interval, Polly's footsteps sounded on the stairs, and then the door was pushed open and the old woman entered, her face pale and slack with fear.

"What is it?" Margaret cried out. "Is it Teresa? Has something happened to Teresa?"

"No, Miss Meg. It's that man. Her uncle. Mr. Salterson." A gnarled old hand tremblingly extended a card to Margaret. "He said to give you this. I put him in the parlor to wait."

Annabelle gave an exasperated cluck, rather like an infuriated kitten, and bounced pettishly upon the bed. "The devil fly away with Uncle Marcus! How like him to come tonight, of all nights, just as I was going to my first party! I vow he's uncanny in the way he chooses the most inconvenient times to call!"

Neither Polly nor Margaret were listening to her. Margaret, her face pale, was reading the card. Beneath his flowing signature he had written,

"Concerning Annabelle Herenford," so there was no use hoping that his visit was merely a wild coincidence.

"He traced me through the inn, no doubt. Daniel would have gossiped about me, and he would be following every lead. But does he know anything else?" She had been shocked back upon her heels, but she was keeping her head.

"If that's all, then he's on a fishing expedition. He can't know anything, Meg." Annabelle was complacent.

"Perhaps not," Margaret said thoughtfully. "But you do understand, don't you, Annabelle, that I can't keep you with me if he knows you are here? The law is on his side."

Annabelle pouted. "Oh please, Meg, try to get rid of him if you can. I do want to go to that party tonight!"

Polly turned on her furiously. "You wicked little girl, you! Is that all you think about? Parties and clothes and your own pleasure? Have you no thought to what Miss Meg has done to herself by keeping you? You tricked her into taking you away from home and yet, if you are found here, you will get off with no more than a scolding from your precious guardian, whereas my Miss Meg can go to prison! And all you can think of is tonight's party, with never a care for her! You are a spoiled, wicked, little——"

"Hush, Polly, hush." Margaret went swiftly to her and laid her fingers on her mouth. "You mustn't blame Annabelle. She did not make me do anything I didn't want to do."

"You felt sorry for her." Tears were rolling down the wrinkled old cheeks.

"Meg." It was a small, abject voice. "Did I do that to you? Put you in danger of prison? Oh, my love, please forgive me! I—I didn't think. But I *was* spoiled and selfish, and had no thought of what I was doing to you by staying here. If I had been thinking of anyone but myself, I would have seen for myself that I—that you were in danger. Please, let me make it right. I shall go downstairs and tell Uncle Marcus the truth about it all and I promise you, he won't——"

"No!" Margaret caught her as she was opening the door, and closing it, faced her tensely. "You won't do it! Not yet! Not until we see what he knows and what he intends to do. Nothing has changed, Annabelle. Have you forgotten your cousin Cedric?"

"I can't let you help me any longer," Annabelle said bravely. "If I beg for Uncle's forgiveness, and promise my aunt that I will marry Cedric without a fuss and that I will be a good girl, I think they will both overlook what I have done, and your part in this."

"No!" Margaret said fiercely. "Do you really want to marry your cousin Cedric, Annabelle?"

The trembling lips and panic-filled eyes were her answer.

"Then leave everything to me. Both of you remain here, and be quiet, unless I call for you to come downstairs."

Halfway down the stairs, she was stopped by the sound of Jodie's piping voice.

"How do you do, sir? My name is Jodie Terrell. My mama is getting dressed for a party, but I will go tell her you are here if you like."

"It isn't necessary," a deep, masculine voice replied. "Your maid has gone to tell her. Come here beside me."

"Did you come from the Rose-and-Crown?" Jodie asked brightly. "Did you notice the stuffed fox behind the counter?"

Mr. Salterson sounded amused. "Yes, I did. Er—does anyone else live here with you? Besides your mother and the maid and you, of course?"

Margaret almost moved then, but Jodie's casual reply stopped her.

"Do you mean Susan?"

"Susan?"

"My cousin, Susan Plunkett. I told her about the fox and she said she would like to see it, because it would be nothing like a puppy. But girls aren't allowed in the common room at the inn. Is that a watch in your pocket, sir?"

"It is." Mr. Salterson sounded resigned, as though a little girl cousin had been lumped into a category with a puppy and a stuffed fox and dismissed. Margaret was smiling as she swept into the room.

Mr. Salterson rose slowly, a startled look on his face. Before him stood a beautiful woman, in a green gown that glimmered and shone in the late afternoon sunlight. Her dark hair had been piled on top of her head in a style that showed her delicate ears and white shoulders and gave her the height she had not had under a bonnet. Green eyes, slightly slanted under finely arched brows, glinted at him with a touch of amusement.

"Jodie." She looked at the little boy. "Run along and allow me to speak to Mr. Salterson alone. Polly laid out your supper in the kitchen." When he had gone, she turned coolly to Mr. Salterson. "What can I do for you, sir? I confess I am—er—intrigued by your message. Who, pray, is Annabelle Herenford?"

Mr. Salterson measured her contemplatively. He had recovered his momentary loss of poise, and Margaret, facing those unexpectedly keen gray eyes, felt a tremor of fear that he could read her mind.

"Madam, I have come for my niece," he said bluntly. "Without roundabation, I know that she is with you, and I expect you to produce her at once!"

"Your niece?" Margaret raised her brows a fraction, giving no hint of her inward shaking. "Do I know your niece, sir?"

"Yes, Mrs. Terrell, you do. You were seen picking her up in your carriage at the crossroads, after you left the inn."

Margaret was jolted and for a fleeting instant it showed in her face, but she made a quick recovery. "You are mistaken, sir. I did not pick up a Miss Annabelle Herenford at the crossroads."

"You lie, madam," he said heavily. "You were seen. My niece was recognized."

"Oh." Margaret was thinking furiously. She suspected that the latter was a shot in the dark—Annabelle could not have been recognized—but nevertheless, the coincidence was too strong. He would expect an explanation of the stranger she had picked up. "I think you are referring to the little governess who was discharged by Lady Maulbrais. I did indeed stop and take her up in my carriage the morning after I met you on the road." She colored. The last was a slip. She had not intended to let him know she remembered him, but she saw from the gleam in his eye that he had caught it, and moreover, that he knew precisely what she meant. "Was she your niece?"

"She is! Lady Maulbrais is also her aunt. She is underage, and anyone giving help to her is subject to prosecution. I expect you to cooperate with me fully," he added in a meaningful voice. "Describe what happened. What did she tell you?"

Margaret described Annabelle in an injured, faintly indignant voice, keeping as closely as possible to the story Annabelle had originally told her. "She wished to take the first coach going to London, so I dropped her at the White Feather." This was a prominent, bustling inn in Chippenham. They had stopped there to change horses and order dinner in one of the private rooms, but so busy was it that she was sure they would not be remembered.

He thought for a moment. "I am sorry, Mrs. Terrell, but I cannot accept that."

"May I ask why not, sir?" she asked indignantly.

"I do not believe that you are the sort of woman who would drop off a child like Annabelle in such a place to fend for herself. Of course, you no doubt know that we made inquiries there and found that no one remembered her, but a woman of your sensibilities would never have abandoned a young girl in the White Feather." She looked uncomfortable, and he went on. "However, Chedworth is on the road to London; a short distance, in fact. It would be in character if you offered her a night's lodging, then put her on the coach the next day. Is that, in fact, what you did? Did she perhaps confide in you, tell you her troubles, and you were sympathetic? Did she tell you where she was going?"

Margaret was on the horns of a dilemma. She was tempted to confirm the story he had just outlined, fleshing it out with a slightly new ending, of course. Where, oh where, could Annabelle have been going? It was much more sensible than her version. But to admit bringing Annabelle here was to bring her uncomfortably close to Susan Plunkett, who would be unmasked if Mr. Salterson started inquiring in Chedworth about strangers.

"Of course not," she said weakly.

"It would be no reflection on you if you gave her help." He was observing her closely. "Her family would be grateful. Perhaps there would even be a reward. No one would blame you if she lied to you about her name and circumstances."

It was, of course, a logical way out, and one that an innocent woman would take. Or a woman with nothing to hide. If she had not already heard of how he was wickedly trying to force Annabelle into a loveless union with her odious cousin, she might be tempted to tell him everything. "This is useless, Mr. Salterson," she said abruptly. "Much as I would like to say I did not, I left your niece in Chippenham. I am sorry, but you must accept that as the truth, unpalatable as it is, and remove yourself from my house. Perhaps your niece will write and reassure you about her whereabouts," she added innocently.

His eyes narrowed. "Now, how did you know that she had done just that, Mrs. Terrell?" he asked softly. "It is, no doubt, a coincidence that I received a letter from her this morning, just before I left London, informing me that she had found a place to stay with the lady in whose carriage she rode when she ran away." Margaret's heart sank, and she silently sent Annabelle to perdition for her garrulity. "She did not want me to worry about her. I already suspected you had given her assistance, and had gone so far as to get your address from your brother-in-law, but this letter confirmed my suspicions. From what you have said today, I believe that you are guilty of not only aiding her, but of encouraging her to to remain away. I warn you, Mrs. Terrell, don't try a fall with me or you'll regret it. Annabelle is a runaway; I am her legal guardian, and you are liable to charges if you have information about her and do not tell it. It could mean a prison term! Once I have lodged an official complaint, the matter is out of my hands. *Now,* do you intend to tell me where I can find my niece?"

She was frightened, but she was careful not to betray her fear to his watchful eyes. "I don't know where she is, and even if I did, I don't like what I have heard—from you and from her. It sounds as though she has been ill-treated or bullied or threatened by Lady Maulbrais, whom I found a most unworthy person, else why should she run away? And why would she not go to you, unless you are in sympathy with Lady Maulbrais's methods? You would have me believe you are solicitous of her welfare. I beg leave to doubt it!"

His eyes slitted with fury. "You are impudent, madam!" he snarled. "What is between my niece and myself—or her aunt!—is none of your business!"

"Precisely, sir!" she snapped. "Because I know nothing about your niece! But I shall make it my business if you bring a constable or any other minion of the law with you. This is *my* village, Mr. Salterson, and your influence doesn't extend here. I am going to a party tonight at the home of the local magistrate, and the constable you threaten me with dandled me on his knee when I was a child! Whom do you think they will believe if you go to them with a tale of my abducting your niece?"

He eyed her speculatively, his former rage having simmered to a deadly calm, which she found more frightening. "By God, you choose to cross swords with me, eh?" he said in a velvety-smooth voice. "I know now, if I did not before, that you have a guilty knowledge of my niece. Your defiance tells me that. I see you have also gauged your own position in the village. But your power doesn't extend beyond it," he added contemptuously, "and I can pluck you out of your village as easily as I would pluck a bug that had the temerity to impede my path. I don't know what your game is—ransom, blackmail, or merely a desire to make mischief—but if I find that you have been playing me false, I will break you, my pretty little lady. I trust this gives you some idea of just how far I will go to win our little battle?"

"I wish you would leave my house at once, Mr. Salterson," she said steadily. "I am going to a party, and I do not want you to continue to remain."

"Good!" he replied coolly. "I shall join you there. The magistrate, you said? I trust that anyone can tell me where he lives?"

She paled. "So you intend to charge me? You have decided upon a confrontation after all?"

"Not at all," he replied evenly. "I have merely decided not to let you out of my sight until you turn up my niece. I shall show up at your party tonight, and if you are not there, God help you."

"But you—can't—just walk in uninvited," she stammered. "What will the Mendenhalls say? How can I explain your presence? Oh—you are mad!"

"You begin to comprehend me," he said smoothly. "As for what your host will say, I will trust you to provide me with an introduction as well as a plausible explanation for my presence."

"I could refuse, you know," she snapped.

"Then, my lady, prepare for that confrontation," he replied grimly. "I don't care what you say—tell them whatever you like, but I expect to attend that party tonight!"

CHAPTER VII

"He's hard, and cruel, and—and pitiless, Annabelle. You were right not to trust him."

The two women were in the parlor with Margaret, who was dividing her time between pacing the floor and returning to peer anxiously out the window. She had watched Mr. Salterson stride angrily off, and she awaited now the arrival of the Mendenhall chaise. There was nothing she wanted to do less than attend a party tonight at Netherwood, but having said she was going, she had to go or draw suspicion upon herself.

"Under no circumstances can you depend upon your uncle," she added sternly. "We must think of something quick, before he comes back here to search this house. And next time he will have a constable."

Annabelle's chin quivered. "W—why does he think I'm here?"

"I don't think he's sure just where you are," Margaret frowned. "I believe he thinks you might be in London, but at the same time he suspects that I know where you are. I am sure he intends to watch me, and this house, to see if I lead him to you. That's why you should get away at once, while I am at the party tonight, for by tomorrow it may be too late. Think. Is there anyone at all you can turn to?"

"Gussie—or Lizzie——" began Annabelle in a small voice.

"Oh, Annabelle, use your head," Margaret said impatiently. "He is going to find out about Susan Plunkett sooner or later, and you simply aren't safe here in Chedworth. You must leave."

"Then the only person I might appeal to is my great aunt Hortense. My grandpapa Salterson's sister. I intended to go to her before you so providentially came along, because she hates Aunt Serena and Cedric. But now," Annabelle added mournfully, "it simply won't do."

"Why do you say that?" Margaret asked quickly.

"Because she is also Uncle Marcus's aunt. I don't precisely know how she feels about him, but I suspect she likes him very well. I could not depend upon her to sustain me in a crisis against him."

Margaret's even, white teeth worried the tip of one finger. "But you don't know?"

"No-o-o," Annabelle said doubtfully.

"When one is in the sort of scrape you are in at the present time, one must grasp at straws," Margaret said determinedly. "Tell me something about her. Where does she live?"

"In Bath. She has a home in Camden Place and lives there year round in order to take the waters. She is immensely wealthy and hates London, and keeps a companion whom she bullies to death. She has come to points with Aunt Serena several times, for she has the reputation of saying whatever she thinks."

Margaret gazed thoughtfully out the window. The Mendenhall chaise rolled to a stop before the gate, and her eyes sharpened on it, with its handsome equipage and the stout, ponderous coachman who pulled the horses to a halt. Annabelle's voice, meanwhile, had trailed to a stop, and she and Polly watched her hopefully. During the past hour, Polly's animosity toward Annabelle had shattered with a crash, for they were all in a common predicament with no one better off than the other. Her Miss Meg's positive assertion that Annabelle's wicked uncle was an ogre, a fiend in human form, a monster who would delight in seeing his niece married against her will, had been an impressive charge, one that turned the tide of her sympathy. She listened, therefore, with a strained attention, ready to interrupt if she thought of anything to suggest.

"I think I have an idea," Margaret announced briskly. "I shall ask Lucian for the loan of the Mendenhall coach, to convey you to Lawton Grange."

"Lawton Grange?" Annabelle asked wonderingly. "What would I be doing at Lawton Grange?"

"Never mind that. I shall think of something. You are my cousin, remember? You have family business there. I shall write a note to Dr. Stockton, explaining everything, and I wager if anyone can protect you from your horrid uncle, it will be he!" She drew out a piece of paper from a desk drawer and dipped her pen in the standish. "As soon as Mr. Salterson gives up and leaves Chedworth, I shall follow and go at once to see your aunt. I shall sound her out on the prospect of hiding you from the rest of your family. Polly, can Nell go along to act as Annabelle's abigail?"

"My sister? Of course," Polly nodded. "She'll do anything for you, Miss Meg. You know that."

"Good. Send Jodie with a message to her cottage, and you help Annabelle pack. I shan't see you again," she added, giving Annabelle a swift kiss, "until I see you at Lawton Grange."

"Meg," Annabelle asked doubtfully, "will Mr. Mendenhall lend you his horses to travel *at night?*"

"Of course he will!" Margaret said stoutly. "Fortunately, there's a bright moon tonight and the coach has side lanterns. He'll think nothing of it!"

Mr. Mendenhall, however, was not so easily persuaded. Despite having been a military man, and not unused to rash decisions ending in brilliant results, he nevertheless favored the most mundane, tried-and-true methods. To lend his coach, coachman, and groom, and more importantly a team of expensive horses, on what seemed to him no more than a harebrained scheme—which had not yet been explained to his complete satisfaction—was to strain to the breaking point his faith in Margaret's good judgment, as well as his wish to please her. She had been forced to invent a crisis at Lawton Grange, which required the services of a family member yet was too urgent to allow the delay of waiting until the following morning. When Lucian pointed out the oddity of sending a seventeen-year-old girl instead of going herself, Margaret was again forced to fall back upon her imagination and slew Jodie down with a putrid sore throat and fever, necessitating her remaining in Chedworth. She grew frantic as Lucian continued to hesitate, for she was anxious to conclude this business so she could go on to explain Mr. Salterson's forthcoming awkward appearance before it actually occurred.

Lucian might have remained obdurate if George had not chosen that moment to make an appearance, looking for Annabelle. He had been sent to the study by Chloe, who had seen Margaret disappear through the door, and he interrupted with the information that the salon upstairs was rapidly filling with guests and followed with an inquiry about Annabelle. Mercifully, it only took one stammered incoherent explanation for George to respond at once with a decisive voice unlike his usual hesitancy. "Sounds serious to me. Of course you'll help all you can, Lucian. She should leave at once, and what's more, I'll go with her."

"What?" Lucian gaped at him.

"Don't you think I should?" he asked reasonably. "Annabelle has old Nell along, so the proprieties will be taken care of, but what with riding at night and the need to hurry, there should be an extra man along for protection."

Lucian regarded his younger brother approvingly. One of his main objections, the care of his horses, had been wiped out with George's offer to go. He could safely leave his cattle in his brother's hands, so in spite of his obvious reluctance, he gave a measured, cautious assent. Margaret relievedly thrust George out the door before turning back to Lucian to deal with her second request.

"Mr. Salterson is a very old friend of ours, Lucian, Robert's and mine. We—er—knew him in Italy. He arrived unexpectedly today to pay his respects. I either had to invite him here tonight or stay at home with him."

"But of course he is welcome, my dear. Need you ask?" Briefly, he dropped an affectionate hand on her shoulder. "Come, now. I must go and greet my guests."

Upstairs, the party was already in full swing. Above the feminine chatter, the clink of glasses and male voices gave away the location of the punch bowl near the doorway, and someone was thumping out an erratic tune on the pianoforte.

Netherwood was an imposing house, with large, handsome rooms filled with rich furniture. The party was being held in the ballroom, which was long and mirrored, with windows at one end overlooking the clipped lawn that swept to the river. At the other, a pair of double doors had been thrown open into an anteroom, where card tables had been set up. Altogether there were slightly more than forty people present—with the ages ranging from fifteen-year-old Chloe to a septuagenarian, who was seated against the wall—and about half of those were young enough to have every intention of dancing. They hailed Margaret with cries of delight, thrusting sheets of music at her, for she was a talented pianist and good-natured enough to play for them without complaining.

She was glancing through the music when a feeling of being watched made her look up. Mr. Salterson was standing in the doorway, studying her critically. He was dressed very properly in evening clothes, but from the bored look on his face, she suspected that he considered the present company a gathering of country nobodies unworthy of his attention. Margaret tensed and returned his look with an icy glare. Fortunately Lucian, who was standing nearby, did not notice, or he might have wondered about her cold reception of an old friend.

He was already striding forward, holding the card his butler had given him and saying warmly, "Lucian Mendenhall, at your service, sir. Mrs. Terrell told me that you were coming, although somehow, from what she said, I expected a doddering ancient," he added dryly.

"I hope that my presence has not inconvenienced you, sir."

"Oh, not at all!" Lucian replied heartily. "We are always glad to see a fresh face at our little county parties. Er—Mrs. Terrell told me that you made the trip especially to pay your respects. An old friend of theirs whom they knew in Europe?"

Mr. Salterson's eyebrows rose slightly. "Europe? Yes, of course," he agreed smoothly. "A *very* old friend."

Somehow, without Lucian quite realizing what had happened, he found himself firmly put aside as Mr. Salterson strolled purposefully across the room toward the pianoforte, and Margaret.

"Europe, madam?" he queried in a savage undertone.

She looked up from her music. He was angry.

"You said to make up my own story," she said defensively.

"And a damned impertinent one it is, under the circumstances. Investing me with the role of an old friend when I cannot even qualify as a friendly enemy!"

"Well, what was I to do?" she demanded. "You thrust yourself upon me unexpectedly and insist that I force my host to accept you as a guest! Was I to tell him the truth? It may surprise you to know it, sir, but I have a great many friends here tonight, and none of them would welcome my enemy! I suggest, if you want to stay here, you follow the story that I have given Lucian; that you are a friend of my husband's whom I knew in Rome five years ago. You will not be questioned too closely, since none of the people here were ever in Rome at that time."

"Now, how would you know that the best lie is

a simple one, Mrs. Terrell?" he asked ironically.

By this time, the young people had formed squares for the first country dance, and Margaret struck up the first chord of music, her only indication that she had heard his words a slightly deeper flush.

"Are you wishing to pick a quarrel with me, Mr. Salterson?" she challenged. "If so, I think you will be disappointed. I cannot give you my undivided attention while playing."

He shrugged. "No, I will allow you this victory since it is a minor one. I wish to ask you a question which you can answer with half your attention on it. Why were you so quick to judge Lady Maulbrais as an incompetent guardian?"

"It was merely a guess on my part," she said hastily. "I met her only once. I know nothing about her."

"Evasive to the end." He smiled sarcastically. "Can you tell me that the little governess did not confide in you? No hint about her aunt-employer? Nor her wicked uncle? No choice morsel that you may now throw into my teeth? I am giving you an opportunity to say what you will, Mrs. Terrell, so where is your courage? Whereby did you gain your opinion of Miss Herenford's aunt? After all, my sister herself placed her child in her care. Doesn't that mean something?"

"Perhaps your sister did not know her very well."

124

"Not know her well! She lived in her pocket for four years! Amelia's husband died of a hunting accident soon after Annabelle was born, and my sister chose to remain with Lord and Lady Maulbrais at Queen's Keep rather than set up her own establishment or return to her own home. No, Amelia knew her and loved her very much."

"Perhaps, then, your sister did not know what love was," Margaret faltered. "An heiress might not, you know. And if one has never known it, one might mistake something else for it."

Mr. Salterson frowned, studying her face intently. "My sister was eight years older than I," he said slowly. "She married when I was a schoolboy. I remember thinking she was making a mistake, for I thought her husband a charming wastrel, but at the same time she was perilously close to being on the shelf, and one marriage was as good as another. It was no easy time for her, for our parents were dead." He might have been talking to himself.

During this time Mr. Mendenhall had been making a determined effort, with the help of his stepmother, who was an avid card player, to shoo those persons who were not dancing into the card room. He had planned the evening carefully, even to the numbers required for the tables, and had intended taking advantage of Mrs. Terrell's preoccupation with the music to remain at her side, turning the pages. However, all was not going as he had hoped. Margaret was deep in conversation with the stranger, and he had found Mrs. Marshbanks, who had been chatting with the vicar, unexpectedly recalcitrant.

She was in a nasty mood. She had noticed Margaret's dress almost at once and had immediately realized that although the material was the same, the style and cut were more elegant than hers. She had seen it as a direct slap in her face, for she remembered distinctly mentioning that she intended to wear green satin. She was unable to draw nearer to study it more closely, for to do so would be to call attention to her own dress's shortcomings; so she was forced to remain at a distance, seething with impotent rage and plans for Mrs. Tompkins's discomfiture.

As the room slowly emptied of card players, she could see Margaret more closely, and for the first time, her companion. Instantly, she was struck with a blinding blow. She recognized Mr. Salterson at once for a very good reason. She had been among a crop of young women making their bow to society, and that season, many had set their caps in vain for the rich Marcus Salterson. Irene remembered vividly the occasion of one snubbing she had received. Her mother, convinced that her daughter's ripe beauty was capable of capturing the pick of the eligibles in spite of her lack of dowry, set as her goal Marcus Salterson and bore down upon him as purposefully as a cat approaching a mousehole. He had already learned to deal with fortune hunters, and he treated them both with a contemptuous indifference that rankled to this day; and what was more mortifying, Irene was certain that he had forgotten her as soon as the incident was closed.

"Upon my soul, isn't that Marcus Salterson?"

Lucian Mendenhall looked over his shoulder briefly. "It is. Now, Mrs. Marshbanks, they are waiting for you in the card room. If you will——"

"I don't think I want to play cards just now." Irene began to waft her fan languidly. "You have my curiosity piqued, Mr. Mendenhall. How did you meet Mr. Salterson? I did not even know you were his friend."

"I am not," Lucian informed her crisply. "He is a friend of Mrs. Terrell's. She met him while in Europe. He visited her here in Chedworth to pay his respects, and she asked my permission to include him in tonight's party."

Irene's eyes narrowed at this astounding piece of news. "I never heard of such a thing! Meg Terrell know the great Marcus Salterson and never give so much as a hint of it! Or Robert either, so far as that goes! No, no, Mr. Mendenhall, Meg Terrell is merely boasting of a friendship that does not exist."

"You are mistaken," Mr. Mendenhall told her

frostily. "Mr. Salterson himself confirmed their friendship as a long-standing one." He moved on, wishing Mrs. Marshbanks to perdition and thinking bitterly that it looked as though he was going to have to join the card players in order to make up the numbers.

The vicar, who never played cards and was therefore absolved from Mr. Mendenhall's animosity, had been watching Irene closely. He said mildly, "I suspect he knew them both while they were in Rome. There is a small, close-knit English colony there, I am told. Who is Mr. Salterson anyway, Mrs. Marshbanks? You seem—er—impressed."

"Oh, he is the great Marcus Salterson." She tittered angrily. "I myself have never been up to his touch, although I have known him slightly since I came out. He possesses one of the largest fortunes in the country, and his birth is most respectable, I assure you. His grandmother was the Duchess of Afton, and his father was the younger son of a noble family. He has even, upon occasion, snubbed the Prince Regent and gotten away with it, because of his moneybags, of course; but nevertheless, that gives you an idea of the power he wields. He owns at least four magnificent houses in different parts of the country, and it is said, keeps a full staff at each of them. He is the leader of his own set, which is addicted to sporting pursuits. He is dressed quite presentably tonight, but most of the time, it is said by some, one can positively smell the stables on him when he enters the room. Not that he cares!" Her mouth twisted viciously. "He is said to be a financial wizard, but I am sure that I don't know if that is true, although everything he touches does seem to turn to gold. In short, sir, he is a most unlikely person to find here. And we are asked to believe that he stopped over to pay his respects to a poverty-stricken little country miss! No, I am sorry, but I can't swallow *that!*" she concluded spitefully.

"Dear me," said Mr. Clavering slowly, "a most impressive accounting. I think perhaps you have made a mistake in your Mr. Salterson, and this one resembles closely the other one?"

"Sir, I am not a fool!" Irene snapped offendedly. "I have seen him many times. And Mr. Mendenhall verifies his name. No, I have made no mistake. The only mistake is his—in believing that he can carry on his games here, in a respectable home! It is obvious why he is here: he apparently has only recently learned that she is available, and that's the reason for his stopover in Chedworth! His reputation is notorious in London, but one would think he would confine his licentiousness to a society that can understand the rules!" Irene was too angry and jealous to remember that she was talking to a man of the cloth who was also a friend of Margaret's. "Now I know the secret of her dress! It was

129

not, after all, made here in Chedworth, but is a direct London import, just as I suspected. And I have been wondering how she could afford it. I fancy we don't have to look too far to find the answer to *that!*"

"Mrs. Marshbanks, you forget yourself," the vicar said icily. "I find your suggestion offensive, and I hope you will not make another accusation of that nature against Mrs. Terrell unless you are prepared to prove it." He rose and moved away, his disapproval apparent in every line of his erect body.

Mr. Salterson was leaning against the wall, his arms folded, idly watching the dancers, when he was startled to find himself addressed by a white-haired old gentleman with kindly blue eyes.

"Mr. Salterson? I am Mr. Clavering, the vicar of this parish. Perhaps you wish nothing more than to be left in solitude, but I wanted to make your acquaintance, sir. I believe you have the honor of knowing an old friend of mine, Margaret Terrell?"

Mr. Salterson inclined his head. "We are merely passing acquaintances," he denied smoothly.

"I thought so." The vicar gazed vacantly over the heads of the dancers. "There is one here who knew you in London, where apparently you bear a somewhat outstanding reputation for amorous exploits." Mr. Salterson frowned slightly, and the vicar hurried on. "I am being impertinent to even mention this, but I assure you, I proceed with the best intentions. Margaret Terrell is like my own daughter, and indeed, since she has no one to protect her name, I suppose I stand as close as anyone to being a guardian of her reputation. The lady whom I mentioned has never been known for discretion, and I do not want Meg hurt by her undeserved slurs."

Mr. Salterson smiled with a certain amount of grim amusement. It had never occurred to him that his reputation, such as it was, would precede him and certainly not that it would recoil on Mrs. Terrell. He wondered ironically if he should propose an exchange to her: information about his niece in return for an open declaration of his disinterest. "I assure you, Vicar, that there is nothing in the least—er—romantic about my interest in Mrs. Terrell. I did, however, come to Chedworth with the express purpose of seeing her, and I may stay on for a while. As for the rest, I suggest that you apply to her for an explanation. She has shown herself perfectly capable of giving one when the occasion demands it."

The blue eyes studied him intently. "I see. I apologize for my mistake. It seems that I have been misled. You will naturally be as wishful as I in having this rumor scotched. In the meantime,

131

if you ever want to hear the truth about Meg Terrell from someone who knows her well, I am at your service."

Mr. Salterson frowned. "I thank you, Mr. Clavering." He seemed about to say more, but stopped abruptly. "Who is that lady across the room who seems to be trying to catch my eye? She looks slightly familiar."

Mr. Clavering did not look around. "That is Mrs. Irene Marshbanks," he said dryly. "She is the one who claims to know you."

"Indeed? Mrs. Terrell's enemy? Then we might have something productive to say to one another. I think I will renew the acquaintance." Mr. Salterson strolled away and a moment later was bowing over Mrs. Marshbanks's gloved hand while she distributed sparkling smiles and looks.

"You naughty, naughty creature," she cried archly, tapping his wrist with her fan. "What are you doing in our isolated little village? Imagine my surprise when I looked up and saw the famous Mr. Salterson! No one had prepared me for your coming nor told me you were here. Just imagine, I was actually thinking of leaving Chedworth because I was bored, but nothing can prevail me to leave now I know you are here! Just sit right down here beside me and tell me what you are doing here, you unexpected man! Is it true that you have known Meg Terrell any time these past five years?"

"You must ask Mrs. Terrell to tell you that. My lips are sealed about the details of our acquaintance." Mr. Salterson had a slightly sour look, as though Mrs. Marshbanks's coyness was wearing thin.

"Now, now Mr. Salterson!" She cocked a rougish eye at him. "You might fool the rest of this crowd with that nonsense, but you forget that I know who you are and know your circle in London! Meg Terrell simply isn't one of them! She never spent more than a fortnight in London and has been a country mouse all of her life. Your interest in that young woman cannot be innocent, and as her cousin and a guardian of her morals, I protest! What do you want with her?" She knew that she was being indiscreet, but she was thrilled with her success in capturing his interest and she had no intention of allowing her prize to get away, even if it meant destroying Margaret's reputation in the process.

He eyed her coolly. Her questioning had been obvious, her double meaning unsubtle. His lips curled. "Why should you question that I knew her in Europe?"

"I am Margaret Terrell's cousin. By marriage. It was in my house that she met Robert Terrell. In fact, in this very house, for Netherwood was my home then. I know all about Meg Terrell's year in Europe, and I know they did not go about in society. Frankly, they could not afford it, because Robert's father had refused him an allowance and they lived on what Meg and her sister received from their mother's estate. A pittance, I assure you."

"I see." She studied his face hungrily, but could learn nothing from his impassive features. "You are quite right. I did not meet Mrs. Terrell in Europe. It is not precisely a secret, but I am not wishful of having my affairs discussed openly, so I asked her to pretend that we were friends to explain my presence here. As you might have suspected, my interest in Mrs. Terrell is a business one. Her name has been suggested as a chaperon for my young niece. What do you think about it? Would she be a suitable person?" He watched her expectantly.

"You can't be serious?"

"Why not?"

"It—it's ridiculous! She's too young! It would be most unsuitable! I presume you *are* speaking of your sister Amelia's child?"

"Precisely."

"Whoever proposed such a strange thing to you? Who could have thought of Margaret Terrell? As well employ that silly little cousin of hers!" Irene's eyes glittered with shock, envy, or perhaps merely sheer malice. "I really don't know if I should take you seriously or if I am supposed to know it is a joke. I will confess that when I saw that gown she was wearing and knew she could never have afforded it, I thought——" She stopped short, biting her lips. "It is beyond anything *if* it is true, and I do not believe for a minute that it is." She gave a sharp, brittle laugh. "I assume, if you are thinking of employing Margaret Terrell, you're looking into her character and virtue?" she asked with exquisite sarcasm.

He raised his eyebrows slightly. "Do I understand from your words that her character is doubtful?"

Irene hesitated momentarily. "It is not for me to say, but rather for my cousin, Lord Buckhaven, who will have much to tell you if you are indeed interested in hearing about Meg Terrell."

Mr. Salterson stared, masking his revulsion with an effort. "What game are you playing, madam?" he asked sharply. "Is her character in doubt or not?"

"I have not said so!" she retreated hastily. "It is for Lord Buckhaven to say. If he wishes me to, I will tell you what I know, but you must allow me a few days to get his permission."

"I have no wish to listen to anything except as it might pertain to my niece's interests," Mr. Salterson said mendaciously. "If you, or Lord Buckhaven, have any information that reflects upon Mrs. Terrell's abilities as a chaperon, I shall be glad to hear about it."

She nodded. "I still can't believe it, but I suppose it came about through that Plunkett child? She and your niece would be about the same age."

He froze. "Susan Plunkett? The little cousin. I—er—don't see her here tonight."

"No, neither do I, and I would have thought wild horses couldn't keep her away." Mrs. Marshbanks laughed spitefully. "I suppose she has the measles."

"Measles?"

"Her entire family in Leeds was prostrated with them, and to hear Susan tell it, she was the only one who remained upon her feet and nursed the rest of them. She doubtless imagines herself some sort of heroine, I fancy, but it all sounds excessively vulgar to me." Irene fanned herself vigorously. "I presume she has finally succumbed to the measles and no doubt infected the whole of the population of Chedworth, too. *I* found her an extremely ill-mannered little chit with a pert manner of speaking, although I've heard others speak of her as a pretty little blond creature wtih passing good manners. Oh! You're not going?" she cried disappointedly.

"Yes, madam, I must speak to Mrs. Terrell."

But he did not get his opportunity at once. He

was forced to bide his time until supper was served, when under cover of bringing her a claret cup, he managed to speak to Margaret alone.

"Your little cousin is not here tonight," he murmured. "The measles, I presume?"

The face that was lifted to his was beautifully innocent, but her voice was fatalistic as she replied, "Susan? Who told you about her?"

"Mrs. Marshbanks. Oh, a veritable harpy, I agree, but a fount of information, nevertheless. Where do you have her hidden, Mrs. Terrell?"

"Oh, she has returned to her home."

"Leeds?" he asked sarcastically. "We shall see, Mrs. Terrell." He added, as Mr. Mendenhall bore down upon them with a plate for Margaret and one for himself, "I shall call upon you tomorrow to discuss her whereabouts, and I hope you won't attempt to fob me off with a tale about Leeds."

CHAPTER VIII

But the bird had flown by the following morning. Margaret had been afraid that Mr. Salterson would set a guard upon the cottage to watch her own movements when he learned that Annabelle was gone, so she left at dawn. She had the advantage of knowing about the bakery cart that made its early morning run to Little Mitford. From there, she could get the London-to-Bath mailcoach after it left Chedworth, and hopefully confound Mr. Salterson's efforts to trace her movements.

Her weak link was Polly. She had given her old nurse instructions to delay Mr. Salterson as long as possible, but she had little hope that the old woman would have the wits to evade his questions for very long. She seemed to have an almost superstitious awe of him, and she was frankly terrified out of her wits. It wouldn't take him long to shake the information out of Polly that her destination was Bath, and once he learned that, he would no doubt immediately think of his aunt. Margaret was frankly pessimistic about her own chances of protecting Annabelle. Her one hope lay with Miss Salterson, an unknown factor as yet, but who might be able to take on her nephew and come out ahead of the game.

By seven o'clock that morning, Margaret was awaiting the coach from the private room of the Pidgeon in Little Mitford and by ten o'clock, they were in Chippenham, where a squally shower overtook them. Their progress was necessarily slowed by the weather; so that by the time they reached Bath, it had settled to a steady rain, they were late, and Margaret's stomach felt as though it had met her backbone from lack of food. The coach lumbered into the city, passing the Old Bridge on its way into the center of town, then turned into Stall Street. Its destination was the White Hart Hotel, which overlooked the Pump Yard and much of the activities involved with those who wished to take the waters. Through its rain-streaked windows, Margaret could see the constant passage of carriages, closed against the rain; and above the noise of their wheels, she heard the rumble of carts and drays, the cries of newsmen, milkmen, muffin men, as they shouted to sell their wares, and as insistent as the tinkle of wind bells, the clink-clink of pattens on the cobbled streets and sidewalks.

One of the hostlers in the bustling inn-yard of the White Hart told her the direction to Camden Place, and then, taking pity on her bewilderment, hailed her a sedan chair. With her slender resources strained to the limit by the coach fare, and now the chairmen's fee, she was not able to afford a meal, so she proceeded directly to Miss Salterson's home. When she knocked and asked admittance, she was dizzy from hunger and lack of sleep, and she did not make a particularly prepossessing picture upon the doorstep, pale and rumpled as she was from her hours in the tightly packed mail-coach. However, Annabelle's name was the magic word needed for the dour manservant to eventually usher her in to Miss Salterson's presence.

Miss Salterson was tiny, with piercing gray eyes and a hawklike nose. Her diminutive size and white hair gave her a misleading appearance of fragility, whereas she was actually every bit as indomitable as granite. Margaret was reminded at once of Annabelle, but even more forcibly of Mr. Salterson. Instead of finding this off-putting, however, it was strangely reassuring.

Miss Salterson, in turn, saw before her a beautiful young woman in a rather shabby dress and bonnet, a young woman who was pale faced and, to her alarmed eyes, seemed to be swaying slightly. The confused, mumbled message that she had come on behalf of Annabelle she thrust aside, in the more immediate concern of preventing a swoon right in front of her on the floor.

"Sit down, my dear," she said quickly, "you look ill. Is something wrong?"

Margaret tried to smile. "Pardon me, ma'am, I am a little tired. I did not sleep last night, and I have been traveling since before five o'clock this morning and came direct to you as soon as I arrived in Bath, for the matter is urgent, and——"

But Miss Salterson was already ringing for a maid and halted Margaret's stumbling explanation until a tray containing coffee, richly laced with cream and sugar, and a plate of macaroon cookies was in front of her. Reviving as she ate, Margaret began to take a little more interest in her surroundings. The drawing room in which she sat was handsomely furnished in elegant style, the wallpaper was silk and the drapes woven of gold thread. Seeing her shiver in her damp clothes, Miss Salterson had quietly ordered the fire to be lit, and Margaret could not help but contrast her kindliness to Lady Maulbrais's grudging hospitality. Miss Salterson's companion, a twittery little creature named Miss Nicholson, had been impatiently dismissed earlier, and now there were just the two of them, with Margaret making inroads on the plate of cookies while Miss Salterson studied her frankly and liked what she saw.

Margaret kept back nothing of her story, for her first objective was to win Miss Salterson to Annabelle's side. She seemed to grasp it all at once, although when Margaret finished, she had a few strangely unrelated questions to ask, such as Margaret's background, as well as her precise relationship to Dr. Stockton. Margaret explained haltingly, and Miss Salterson nodded briskly.

"Melissa Stockton almost died of the vapors when that brilliant son of hers became a surgeon. I understand he is, famous throughout the world now. Is he in love with you?" she asked abruptly.

The question was too frank for Margaret to take offense. "No, ma'am," she replied tiredly, "he is merely a good friend. And would do anything he could do to help me, I know. He has tried to prevent me from paying his fees, but I would not allow Tessa to stay on charity."

Miss Salterson nodded, then added casually, "You know that Marcus will be sure to come here, either by tracing you or because I am just about the only person to whom Annabelle might turn?"

"Yes, ma'am, but you will keep her, won't you? You will allow her to stay with you? Please?"

"Oh, I certainly shall try to prevent him from turning her over to that wretched woman and her

142

son; but you do know that I cannot keep her with me if he chooses to insist? After all, she is his ward, not mine." She watched closely as a range of emotions swept Margaret's face, the last of which was determination.

"You're right, of course, ma'am. You *are* helpless, and may fear to confront him. I can understand that. But if you will offer to take her in, give him that choice, then I will undertake to prevent him from removing her."

"You seem convinced that he intends to see her married to Lord Maulbrais?" Miss Salterson asked curiously. "Is he so inconsiderate of her feelings?"

Margaret flushed. "Not altogether, ma'am. I would hate to malign your nephew, for you may be fond of him. But I wish to inform you that he is pigheaded, obstinate, bad-tempered, and autocratic, and would do anything to get his own way merely because he dislikes to be bested!" Margaret snapped. "He has yet to learn that he is not always right in everything he says or does!"

A muscle twitched in the corner of Miss Salterson's cheek. "Ah? My dear Margaret, if I may call you that? You are, I think, *precisely* the person to talk to him. I give you leave to do so. It will do him a great deal of good to learn that he is not universally admired by every woman he meets."

Margaret's eyes sparkled. "Certainly not, ma'am!" she said emphatically.

"Just so." Miss Salterson's gravity seemed threatened. "In the meantime, we must be practical. If I am allowed to keep Annabelle, what am I to do with her? Marcus is sure to point out that I am too old to keep up with her as I ought. Therefore, I intend to suggest that he allow you to take over the task of helping me until we can make other arrangements."

Margaret looked dismayed. "Oh no, ma'am, please, I—can't." Under Miss Salterson's inquiring eyes, she explained miserably. "My clothes—I only brought a few things with me—and I don't have——"

"Oh." Miss Salterson's face cleared up. "Naturally, the necessary clothes will be furnished. That is understood. By me," she added, as Margaret continued to look mulish. "Marcus will have nothing to do with any arrangements I make with you, and of course, *I* expect to pay you a salary. All very businesslike. In fact, I don't intend to allow you or Annabelle to stir a step until we've attended to the matter of new clothes. Now, does that answer your objections? Come, come, my girl, where is your spirit of adventure?"

"He'd never consent to it," Margaret said hesitantly.

"We'll see." Miss Salterson's eyes sparkled. "You must leave some things to *me!* Now, I'll have Mulroyd summon my chaise, and you may go to

Lawton Grange and bring Annabelle back to me. I don't think my nephew will tarry long behind you, and I would not like to receive him alone."

However, before Margaret could rise, there was a discreet tap at the door, and Mulroyd, looking harried, informed his mistress that Miss Annabelle was here with a young gentleman.

Annabelle entered with a rush and flung herself, weeping, into Margaret's lap, while George looked anguished. When Margaret informed her briskly that her aunt was willing to have her, she then transferred herself to Miss Salterson's narrow lap and wept some more. Margaret, who was beginning to suspect that Annabelle was thoroughly enjoying herself, prosaically said that she might as well save some tears until later, when they might be useful in the talk she could expect to soon have with her uncle. Annabelle sat up at once, dried her eyes, and entered into the practicalities of their situation. As Margaret suspected, George had been told everything, and he earned Annabelle's limpid gratitude and Miss Salterson's grudging approval by saying stoutly that he did not intend to forsake Annabelle in her hour of need; that whatever his brother might say, he intended to remain in Bath, and to that end, had already dispatched old Nell home in his brother's coach, along with a message, carried by the coachman, informing him of his intention. He had rented for himself also an adequate pair of horses and a curricle, and with these he intended returning to Lawton Grange, now that Annabelle was settled, and getting their luggage. After that, he would see about a pair of rooms at the White Hart. He was agreeable to taking Margaret with him, for she felt that not only was an explanation due to Dr. Stockton, but that it might be wise to leave Annabelle alone with her aunt for a while.

As George rounded up the luggage, Dr. Stockton listened to Margaret's explanation with a grave expression on his engagingly homely face. She could not be sure how he was taking it, until she noticed a twinkle in his blue eyes.

"Kind, generous Meg," he mocked gently. "You can't say no, can you?"

"Well, I——"

"Never mind. I shan't even scold you for embroiling me in the crime of aiding a runaway heiress. I shall merely be thankful that at last the child is under the wing of her aunt, who if not her guardian, is at least officially recognized as one of her legal protectors. If I had known the real story, however, I might have been less—er—positive with that top-lofty gentleman when he called upon me." He grinned. "I am too happy today to give you the lecture you deserve."

146

"Happy?"

"Teresa. There has been a breakthrough, my dear," he said simply. "She has begun to remember David and the baby, and her mind accepts the memory and the pain. Accepts and does not reject it as she once did. She is definitely getting well. I think that knowing she has my love has helped." His eyes were shy. "Have I your blessing, Meg?"

For answer, she laid her hand in his outstretched one. "Thank you."

"I have been offered a chair at a school of medicine in Vienna. Now that the Little Corsican has been safely put away—for the second time!—it will be a pleasant place to live. I hope to take Teresa with me, as my wife, if she continues to improve. Wait a few weeks and then perhaps she can tell you about it herself."

George eyed Margaret curiously as she came out of the hospital and got into the curricle. "Good news?"

She smiled and nodded. George, like everyone else, knew that her sister was a patient at Lawton Grange, and of the wonderful results Dr. Stockton had had with some of his patients. But he did not know the whole story, nor of her plight when she returned from Rome with a baby, and a sister who had to be confined to a mental hospital after a long,

147

downhill slide into madness. And of course no one could guess the thrill she felt when she heard Dr. Stockton's prognosis for Teresa's recovery.

She forced herself to reply composedly, and tried to listen intelligently to George, who was full of excited plans for the next few weeks in Bath away from the eagle eye of his older brother. His enthusiasm had her smiling as she stepped from the curricle and made her way into Miss Salterson's house. She was feeling wonderful and she thought triumphantly, *Fie upon you, Mr. Salterson, you no longer have any power to frighten me!*

Miss Salterson's butler would have begged to differ with her when he answered the imperious knock that resounded throughout the house. It was only a few minutes after he had answered the door to the pleasant young lady who was staying here with his mistress.

"That woman who just entered," Mr. Salterson gritted through clenched teeth. "Is she staying here?"

Mulroyd nodded dazedly. He knew his mistress's nephew, of course, and had always considered him the most amiable of gentlemen. This man standing before him, seething with fury, bore little resemblance to his former impression of him.

"Kindly present this card to her and ask her to give me a few minutes of her time," he snarled, so fiercely that Mulroyd stepped back a pace or two.

"You—you—don't wish to see Miss Salterson, sir?" he quavered.

"No!" Mr. Salterson snapped. "My business with my aunt can wait. Just now I wish to speak to Mrs. Terrell!"

Mulroyd showed him into the drawing room, then withdrew to inform Miss Salterson and her two guests that Mr. Salterson was here and wished to speak to Mrs. Terrell and no one else, and that he ventured something had happened to overwrought him. By this, the ladies rightly understood that Mr. Salterson was in a flaming temper.

"Well." Margaret squared her shoulders. "I'd better go and see him."

"We'll give you five minutes alone with him," Miss Salterson told her solemnly. "Then we'll come and rescue you."

Mr. Salterson looked up at her entrance and glared at her. She had removed her bonnet and fluffed her hair, but her face, no longer shadowed by the bonnet's brim, was pale and vulnerable. Mr. Salterson's early arrival had shaken her. She could almost credit him with the luck of the devil, to have traced her this quickly.

"Well, madam," he exploded. "I have run you to earth like the vixen you are! Don't deny that my niece is here!"

"Of course I don't deny it," she said placidly.

"It would be foolish to try to do so. She and Miss Salterson will be in shortly, if you care to sit down and wait."

"By God, madam, but you have a nerve!" he gasped. "I never expected such brazen effrontery! You actually admit that you stole my niece from her home, allowed me to spend a week searching for her, and then have the gall to act as though nothing had happened!"

"Naturally, I do not admit such a thing," she said indignantly. "If we are to have a discussion on the subject—and we must, I suppose, since you are obviously dying to quarrel with me—let's not begin it by distorting the facts! I admit that I am responsible for Annabelle being here in her aunt's house, but I said *nothing* about stealing her from her home."

His face darkened with anger. "You are indulging in sophistry, Mrs. Terrell! You encouraged Annabelle to evade her guardians; you deliberately concealed her presence in your home, where she lived under the name of Susan Plunkett; and when I got too close, you took her, or sent her away; in fact, your crimes are too numerous to mention," he asserted sternly, "and if I dealt with you as you deserve, I would have you arrested and thrown into jail, right here in Bath. If you remember, Mrs. Terrell," he reminded her curtly, "I told you that once you stepped outside your own village, you would lose your power over me. Now I demand that you bring Annabelle here at once, and then take yourself out of my aunt's house and Annabelle's life forever."

She listened to him calmly. "What are you going to do with her?"

He leaned across the table and balanced himself on the tips of his fingers. "That, Mrs. Terrell, is none of your business!" he snapped.

"Then I shan't allow her to come in until I am sure what you intend to do about her marriage to Lord Maulbrais," she replied coolly.

"*You* shan't allow her to come in! *You!* Young woman, *you* have nothing to do with it! This isn't your house!" he added furiously.

"How do you do, Marcus?"

His aunt, followed by Annabelle, sailed gently into the room and took a chair, one of the spindle-legged ones with a straight back. From there, looking like a regal duchess, she smiled sweetly at him and held out her hand to be kissed.

"How do you do, Aunt Horry?" he muttered, taking her hand and bowing over it with punctilious courtesy.

"What do you think of my scheme to keep this naughty child with me for a while?" she asked blandly. "Particularly if I can prevail upon Mrs. Terrell to remain with me and take her to the Assembly Rooms and such, when I don't feel quite like making the effort? A sort of quasi-chaperon for Annabelle?"

"I am sorry, Aunt Horry," he said repressively, "but it won't do. Annabelle is going with me, and as for Mrs. Terrell——" He stopped, with an expression as though he had just bitten down upon something very unpleasant, and added meaningfully, "Mrs. Terrell will not do, either!"

"I'm not going with you, Uncle Marcus," Annabelle announced. If a kitten had turned into a spitting cat, he could not have been more surprised. She had scuttled in behind her aunt, as though scared to death, and taken a chair near Margaret, but now she stood up and faced him defiantly. "I don't intend to marry my cousin Cedric. I don't intend to return to Queen's Keep. I want to stay right here with Aunt Horry and Margaret."

He flushed angrily, but waited impassively until she had finished. Then, as though she had not spoken, he said sternly, "Annabelle, go to your room and get your things. You have been disobedient, and caused me a great deal of trouble and anxiety, and you shall be punished. However, I do not intend to see you married against your will to anyone, and certainly not to your cousin Cedric; nor will you be going back to Queen's Keep, nor live with your aunt Serena. You are coming with me to London, to my house, where I will see you

152

put under the care of a strict governess whose first order will be to curb that willfulness of yours."

"I don't think you listened to me, Uncle," Annabelle replied. "I am not going away and leaving Margaret. She has been kind to me, and Aunt Horry has offered to allow me to stay here and attend some balls and parties. I never attended a party—no, nor a ball, either—in my life, for you spoiled the one at Netherwood for me, just as Aunt Serena did the ones in London. Now I have a chance to do some of the things I have always wanted to do, and for the first time, I shall enjoy it, with Margaret as my chaperon. I don't intend to be taken back to London and locked up like a disobedient child, and if you try to, I shall bite, scratch, and scream, until——"

"I have no intention of indulging you by joining you in an unmannerly brawl," he interrupted contemptuously. "I do expect, however, to remove you from this house, just as I said." He took out his watch. "I shall give you precisely five minutes to do as I told you."

"And when you get me home," Annabelle continued rapidly, "I shall run away, again and again! And each time I shall make such a scandal that you will be sick of me and wish you never heard of me——"

"That, too, can be dealt with." He had not taken his eyes off his watch.

"Oh, I know how you expect to deal with it!" Annabelle cried passionately. "Imprisonment, with a governess who is no better than a female warder! *At my age!* And some day, if I am very, very good, I shall be married off conveniently to some horrid creature even worse, perhaps, than Cedric!"

"You shall not be, as you put it, jailed with a warder," he said briefly, but his mouth quivered as though he was restraining an impulse to laugh. "That is not how I expect to keep you on your best behavior, either now or in the future. If you do not return with me quietly and without fuss," he added deliberately, "I shall swear out a warrant before the local magistrate for Mrs. Terrell's arrest, charging her with child stealing. You are a minor, and she can receive a prison term for what she has done."

"No!" cried Annabelle furiously. "She did not steal me from Queen's Keep! I left on my own and lied to her about who I was. She did not know the truth until the next day, when I begged her not to send me back. You can't be so—so *fiendish* as to punish her for that! I shall tell the judge the truth."

"You won't be allowed to tell him anything," he said suavely. "*I* shall be the one prosecuting her, and I merely have to say that she didn't send for your guardian once she learned who you were. That, in itself, is enough—a crime. No judge can

154

fail to imprison her on that testimony. You now have two minutes left, by the way."

"Meg? Can he do that to you?" Annabelle showed her a stricken, peaked little face. "Was Polly right after all? Can he have you put in prison, in spite of anything I might say?" She burst into tears.

"Look at what you're doing!" Margaret stormed at him. "Look at her face! Are you satisfied with your handiwork, sir?" She clasped the sobbing Annabelle in her arms and faced Mr. Salterson scornfully. "You are wicked, cruel, and unfeeling! Do you enjoy making *children* unhappy? All you want to do is dispose of her with the least inconvenience to yourself, so that you can go back to your *jauntering* life! She has tried to tell you what it means to her to stay in Bath, but all you can do is look at your watch and tick off the time like a—a metronome!"

Mr. Salterson snapped his watchcase shut and returned it to his pocket. "Your tears do not affect me, Annabelle," he said ironically, "and your time is up. Get your cloak. I shan't wait on you a minute longer."

Annabelle, drooping, started to move toward the door, but Margaret clung to her. "No!" she raged. "I shan't let her go! I call your bluff, Mr. Salterson!" She snapped her fingers. "You have been threatening me with arrest since you met me, so I say—*now*, sir—do it! Produce your constables! Remove me in manacles from this house if you dare."

Mr. Salterson surveyed her meditatively. "You mean it?" he said slowly.

"I do!" Margaret, by now, was almost dancing with rage, in direct proportion to his cooling off. "I shan't allow you to push her around any more, as though she was nothing but a piece of—of luggage!"

Miss Salterson, watching in fascinated silence, saw a spasm of exasperation cross his face at this simile. "Annabelle and you, between you, Mrs. Terrell, have invested me with the trappings of the most black-hearted villain of all times," he said sarcastically. "Someday I would like to know just what she told you about me. Do you play chess, Mrs. Terrell?" he added mockingly. "If not, it is a game at which I am certain you would excel. You have successfully checkmated me. You know that I wish to keep down scandal, and have judged just how far I will go to prevent this escapade of Annabelle's from becoming public property. I certainly cannot see myself removing you, or Annabelle—in manacles, or screaming, scratching, and I think, biting?—from this house or any other. So we will let things go on as they are for a while, little one." He smiled at Annabelle with such charm that Margaret caught her breath and saw, for the first time, what had given him his position as the most eligible man in society. "Aunt Horry," he turned to his aunt, the smile still lingering in his eyes, "I regret that this brangling had to occur before you. You must have been both bored as well as disgusted—"

"I assure you, Marcus, I haven't been in the least bored," Miss Salterson said with perfect truth.

"If you will then let Annabelle and Mrs. Terrell remain with you for a while, we will allow Annabelle her partying in the mild waters of Bath society, and see how things go. As for you, Mrs. Terrell——" He turned to her mockingly, his eyes as cold as gray marbles, and Margaret, still stunned over his sudden capitulation, noticed how implacable his face looked once that charming smile had faded. "——you have, I assume, professed a willingness to chaperon Annabelle, which seems to preclude a knowledge of just what you are about. Well, I beg leave to doubt it. You have never known what it was to guide an heiress in society, and although Bath is not London, neither is it Chedworth. You will need to keep your wits about you if you are to avoid the shoals of social disgrace. I shall be interested to see just how you go on."

"Does that mean, then, that you intend to

remain in Bath, Marcus?" Miss Salterson asked with a hidden, amused twinkle.

"But certainly, ma'am," he replied promptly. "I wouldn't miss it for the world."

CHAPTER IX

When Marcus Salterson spoke of the delicacy of
the task of guiding an heiress through the bewildering maze of polite society, he spoke from
a cynical knowledge of his world. It was a knowledge that was not shared by Margaret Terrell,
whose experience was limited to the winter Assemblies at Little Mitford and a single week, when
she was fifteen, spent at Bath, while Vicar and
and Mrs. Clavering took the waters. She knew,
however, that Mr. Salterson would take a malicious pleasure in watching her floundering out of
her depth, and that the only reason he had agreed
to Miss Salterson's request was in order to give
her enough rope to hang herself.

His aunt, entertaining the same doubts, nevertheless had her own reasons for wishing to see Margaret come off well in her encounters with her nephew. She decided, therefore, that it might be well to bestir herself and accompany Margaret on her duties until she had learned her way. She had no great love of sitting against the wall all evening and playing chaperon, but the situation promised some unexpected twists and—if today was anything to go by—might prove highly entertaining. However, she waited to speak her mind until she was alone with her long-time maid, Moxon, and her companion, Sarah Nicholson. It was the habit of the three elderly women to have a cup of hot water drawn from the Bath Pump and a digestive biscuit before retiring, and tonight was no exception, although the time was partially given over to a thorough scrutiny of Miss Salterson's wardrobe, which had been allowed to become sadly depleted.

"Annabelle's clothes will be taken care of as soon as Pendleton arrives in Bath with her trunks. I understand that we have Meg Terrell to thank for her present pleasing appearance, since That Woman has the clothes sense of a blind mare. As for me, I don't think we have to resort to *that*, Moxon!" Through her quizzing glass, she surveyed a limp, purple crepe, trimmed with lilac lace, before waving it aside with a shudder. "It is most important, however, that Meg make a good impression. No woman, however beautiful, can fail to be enhanced by pretty clothes, and moreover, I have plans for her."

Since Miss Salterson had not been backward about confiding these plans, Miss Nicholson, listening with twittering interest, knew precisely what they were, as did Moxon.

"It is time Marcus was getting married, and unless I miss my guess, Margaret Terrell is just the woman for him. If he is allowed to go on in that impossibly selfish fashion of his, he will either become a confirmed bachelor, or what is worse, wind up bringing laced mutton into the family!"

"Horry!" Miss Nicholson gasped, although whether at the vulgarity of the term or the horror of the idea it was hard to say.

"You know it's possible, Nickie." Miss Salterson pursed her lips disapprovingly. "He is thirty-five, acquires one mistress after another, and has shown absolutely no interest in finding a wife among suitable women of good character, simply because he is too comfortable with the status quo. Many men his age marry a girl who can be molded into the kind of wife they want, but Marcus would be bored to the murdering point within a fortnight with the stupid inanities of such a chit. But I noticed today that however infuriated he became, he was not bored with Margaret!" Her eyes crinkled with laughter. "She is *precisely* the woman for him."

"She has no dowry," Miss Nicholson pointed out hesitantly, with all the practicality of a woman to whom money had always had to be the first consideration. "He can look higher for a wife."

"Oh yes, indeed," Miss Salterson agreed comfortably. "Marcus can look as high as he likes for an alliance, if *that* is his consideration. But it isn't. And he need not be deterred by a wife's lack of fortune or even her lack of a respectable portion."

"Money usually marries money," Miss Nicholson sighed.

"Usually," Miss Salterson agreed dryly, "because the rich are the most suspicious people in the world. They distrust everyone—except sometimes their own kind. I should know, since I have been a fool in my time. Now, if I can overcome Marcus's suspicions of her motives and Margaret's dislike of him, they may come to see for themselves that they suit one another very well." She tapped her quizzing glass against her cheek thoughtfully. "No matter what *they* think, *I* like the match and shall see to it that it comes about."

But her plan seemed fated to die before it could be launched, for Mrs. Terrell's antagonism continued unabated, equalled only by Mr. Salterson's unyielding determination to distrust her. Miss Salterson was given several opportunities to witness their mutual dislike, since in spite of the sparring that occurred whenever they met, her nephew continued to drop in at the house at Camden Place frequently. It was precisely this that convinced Miss Salterson that it would be wrong to give up hope.

Another frequent visitor, and one who worried Margaret, was George, who was suffering from an excess of puppy love for Annabelle. Close observation convinced her that Annabelle regarded him more in the light of a brother, but Margaret felt responsible for George, knowing that she had done him no favor if she had put him in the way of contracting a lasting passion.

Therefore, George was underfoot at Camden Place almost every hour of the day until Mr. Salterson took strong measures to fill in his leisure time in such a subtle way that the young man himself did not realize how it happened. George told the ladies about it on Wednesday when he came to tea.

Filling his plate with finger sandwiches and fruit cake, he explained about the accidental meeting with Mr. Salterson that had occurred at the entrance of the White Hart as George was leaving the hotel.

"He thanked me for the care I had taken of his ward—that's you, poppet," he grinned at Annabelle. "Then asked if I'd care to stroll along to the

163

stables to see a matched pair of grays he had just bought. Lord Ogilvie was selling his stables, and Mr. Salterson had happened to hear of it before they went on public auction. Regular sweet steppers they were! Lucian would have been green with envy to see them!"

He enthused about the horses for a few minutes until Annabelle broke in impatiently, wishing to know exactly what her uncle had said to George. "For if he has threatened you, or told you to leave town, I shall have something to say to him about it!" she promised darkly.

"Oh Lud, no, nothing like that!" George said hastily, his mouth filled with cake. "Couldn't have been nicer." Later, George had learned from the bootblack at the White Hart what a remarkable act of condescension it had been for Mr. Salterson to take his arm and stroll all the way down Stall Street with him. His stock had risen considerably at the hotel as a result, and he had no intention of allowing Annabelle to hint that her uncle was anything other than the kindest of gentlemen. "Invited me to dinner that night." George saw no reason to inform the ladies and particularly Miss Salterson what her nephew had said as he issued the invitation: that he wished company, because Bath—on a Tuesday evening with nothing but card Assemblies and old biddies in the Rooms —was dull as ditch water. His rueful grin, admitting George into the brotherhood of gentlemen who must find other means of occupying their time, had been as heady as the champagne at dinner.

It, too, had been lavish, the best the York House could offer. Loin of veal, followed by cold partridges, dressed crab, glazed ham, and what George considered a bewildering array of side dishes, all ending in a flaming, brandied-peach dessert and champagne. "But the best part of the evening was that it put me in the way of meeting Freddy."

"Freddy?" Annabelle asked in an ominous voice.

"Freddy Warburton. He was a guest for supper along with Lord Arkwright, Sir Benjamin Tennison, and Lord Carlyle."

"A dissolute set of rakes," Miss Salterson said firmly.

"Oh no, ma'am," George protested, holding out his cup for a second pouring of tea. "Very agreeable gentlemen, but I could see right away that Freddy and I were out of their class. And when they proposed cards and Freddy suggested that we leave, I was more than happy to oblige, although a trifle fearful that I might offend our host. But Freddy assured me that he would not expect us to stay. They play for high stakes, and he would know that it was above our touch. We went on to a cockfight which was rather dull, but Freddy met up with another chap whom he knew, and before I knew it, a bet was on that Freddy couldn't break the record for the Bath-to-Chippenham run. We are to start in one hour, and I am blowing the tin for him. That is why I came by, to tell you that I wouldn't be seeing you tonight." George finished his tea with a gulp.

Margaret's lips tightened as she sipped her tea and listened. Had she brought George to Bath only to have him meet up with undesirable company, fostered upon him by Mr. Salterson as a subtle form of revenge upon her? At the first opportunity she had of being alone with him, which was the following day, she took him to task over it.

"He is new to Bath and was at loose ends. A youngster like young Mendenhall soon grows bored of dancing attendance upon the ladies all day," Mr. Salterson said smoothly, "so I put him in the way of meeting Freddy. There's not an ounce of vice in Freddy, and he'll make your George a worthy guide around Bath."

"Indeed? Racing on public roads? Cockfights? Painting flagpoles? What other forms of wildness does he have up his sleeve to introduce George to?" she asked furiously.

"If you think a few cockfights and races qualify as debauchery, my dear, then you know nothing of the matter," he said dryly. "The boy is nineteen and has been kept under his older brother's thumb far too long. He is entitled to a few larks, and he is fortunate to have Freddy Warburton as his companion. Freddy will not introduce him to the gaming tables or the women who sell their favors. There, he might indeed come to grief. Besides, why should *you* feel responsible? I understand his brother is in town. Hasn't he called?"

"He left his card this morning," she said stiffly.

"No doubt breathing fire that you were staying in Bath?" he added idly.

"Not at all," she answered loftily. "Lucian brought word from the vicar that all is well at home and that I may stay for a while with a clear conscience, so if you were hoping for me to leave, I am afraid that you are going to be disappointed."

"Is Mendenhall in love with you?" he asked abruptly.

She bridled indignantly. "I can't see that it is any of your affair," she said icily.

He shrugged. "I understand from George that he remains in Bath because of both of you. He has already been to the Pump Room and put his name down in Mr. King's Subscription Book."

"Is that where you get your information?" she demanded. "From George?"

He looked amused. "The lad is unhappy that his brother has come to Bath. He is hoping that you will provide a diversion."

She glared. Mr. Salterson had come too close to the truth to be comfortable. Lucian had tried to persuade her to leave, using every argument at his command, and it was only when he realized that she could not be swayed that he announced his intention of remaining too.

As for Miss Salterson, she was pleased to welcome the newcomer when she learned of her nephew's lack of enthusiasm. As yet, they had made no sallies into the outer world. The arrival of Pendleton with Annabelle's trunks confirmed Miss Salterson's belief that That Woman was utterly devoid of taste, and had shown up the inadequacies of her wardrobe so woefully that several urgent shopping trips to Milsom Street were necessary before she could be presentable. Moreover, there were herself and Margaret to be considered.

The post every morning was filled with invitations, although Miss Salterson rightly attributed this distinction to the presence of an heiress in their midst. Therefore, it was not unexpected that their first evening attendance at the Pump Room would create a flurry of interest. It was a concert in the Octagon Room and their escort was Lucian, whose tall, fair looks caused a certain amount of speculation among the ladies present. There was a buzz as they were guided into their seats, and at the first break in the performance, friends and acquaintances of Miss Salterson pressed forward to greet her.

Margaret found the evening agreeable and not in the least frightening, since Annabelle behaved very prettily and did not give her a moment's worry. In fact, Miss Salterson was the only one who found the evening a bore, for her nephew had not seen fit to come. Although she was disappointed, she was by no means discouraged.

She was expecting some positive results from their next appearance, the following night, at the Dress Ball in the Assembly Rooms. For the occasion, she was wearing gray silk and all her diamonds, and had dressed Annabelle in primrose with an overskirt of Michelin lace and knots of matching ribbons falling from a posy beneath the high bosom. It was Margaret who proved unexpectedly stubborn by refusing to accept a ball gown and insisting upon wearing the green satin made by the village dressmaker. However, when Miss Salterson saw it, she knew that it could not be improved upon, unless by the addition of the Salterson emeralds. Margaret balked here too, but after a great deal of persuasion, was prevailed upon to wear them, although she felt uncomfortably as though she were presenting herself in false circumstances.

The ball was under way when they made their entrance and were greeted by Mr. King and shown to prominent seats at the edge of the floor. Lucian was Margaret's first partner for a country dance, and as they were making the sets, she saw Mr. Salterson across the room. He was attired properly in a long-tailed coat and knee smalls but, being Mr. Salterson, he somehow managed to look disheveled. His necktie had been negligently tied, and his hair looked as though he had been running his hands through it. His appearance was all the more noticeable since he was standing beside a gentleman who, turned out in exquisite fashion, had paused in the act of taking a pinch of snuff to stare, open-mouthed, at Margaret.

Suddenly conscious that she was returning his stare, she looked away hastily and did not allow her eyes to wander for the rest of the dance. At its conclusion, Lucian led her back to her place beside Miss Salterson. Unfortunately, it was already occupied by Lady Maulbrais. Her appearance was unexpected since no one had known she was in Bath.

The two women seemed to be conversing in amiable tones, but Margaret was not fooled. Annabelle was too rich a prize for Lady Maulbrais to give up without a struggle.

Her ladyship greeted her with a thin, sour smile.

"Your timely appearance that rainy day turned out to be a fortunate one for you, didn't it, Mrs. Terrell?" she remarked frostily. "A young woman without references—about whom we have no previous knowledge—but obviously living in reduced circumstances, turns up in an opportune manner and makes herself available to a susceptible young lady like my niece, and *voila!*—the next thing we hear is that she is in Bath, consorting with persons above her own station, occupying an enviable position as a chaperon to an heiress!"

Margaret darted a quick look at Miss Salterson, who nodded serenely.

"Oh yes," she said tranquilly, "I had to tell Lady Maulbrais about our arrangement with you. She expressed such deep concern for my advanced years and my aging health that I had to assure her that the actual duties of chaperon would be undertaken by you, Margaret."

"A woman about whom we know nothing!" spat Lady Maulbrais.

"*I* can give her an excellent reference," Lucian said fiercely. He had been stopped from leaving by her ladyship's first biting words.

Lady Maulbrais raised her quizzing glass. "I

don't believe I gave you permission to address me, young man," she remarked haughtily.

"I don't need permission to defend a friend of mine from a vicious attack!" he replied in an equally cold voice.

Her eyes dancing, Miss Salterson started to perform the introduction but was prevented by Lady Maulbrais. "*I* did not ask to have this—this—*person*—known to me," she snapped. "I must beg you, madam, do not go on with this introduction! At some other time he might attempt to presume upon the acquaintance and that, I assure you, would be intolerable."

"Oh, I don't think a friend of the Iron Duke's would find it necessary to—er—claim your acquaintance, Serena," Miss Salterson said gently. "Indeed, he might rightly fear that *you* might presume."

Lady Maulbrais reddened. "The Iron Duke?" she said weakly. "I—of course—if someone had told me that you were a military man of distinction, I would have——"

"You would have hesitated before insulting me!" Lucian finished for her. "If you have a complaint about Mrs. Terrell, take it up with Mr. Salterson. His back is broad. But do not vent your spleen upon this lady here, who has done nothing to merit your censure."

A high flush mottled her ladyship's cheekbones.

She rose jerkily and left them without another word, but her tight lips and angry eyes warned them that although she might have temporarily quit the field, she had not given up the fight.

"Perhaps you ladies might care for a cup of punch to wash the bad taste out of your mouths?" Lucian suggested.

"A famous suggestion," commented Mr. Salterson, appearing suddenly beside them. He had apparently overheard Lucian's parting words. He was accompanied by the gentleman who Margaret had noticed earlier staring at her.

"Sir Benjamin Tennison wishes to be known to you, Aunt Horry." He added smoothly, "But I must warn you that his real purpose is to seek an introduction to Mrs. Terrell."

Sir Benjamin had very agreeable manners, but he was also determined. Before Margaret knew it, she was dancing the next waltz with him. His objective was to entertain her, and he was successful. She had not been the most popular girl in Chedworth without learning to recognize the symptoms of a gentleman who was charmed with his companion, but she had not expected to encounter it in one of Mr. Salterson's sophisticated friends. Before they finished, he had asked permission to call, and returned her reluctantly to Miss Salterson.

Obviously Lucian had come and gone, for Miss

Salterson was sipping her punch and Mr. Salterson was holding Margaret's cup, which he handed to her without a word. Noticing an odd look on Miss Salterson's face, she wondered uneasily what was amiss.

"Mrs. Terrell, will you do me the honor of the next dance?" Mr. Salterson asked.

He wasn't smiling; in fact, he looked as though the honor was an unpleasant duty.

"Of course, sir, if you will allow me to finish this punch. I am thirsty."

"Certainly," he replied coldly, and Margaret realized that something had happened to make him very angry. With her. "I see you take your chaperon duties very seriously, Mrs. Terrell," he added ironically.

She started. "Where is Annabelle?" she asked guiltily, looking around.

"She is quite safe with Mr. Mendenhall. Now."

Margaret wondered confusedly if this could be the reason for his anger, but then she thought she understood when he turned to his friend, Sir Benjamin, and added, "I hope your waltz with Mrs. Terrell was as pleasurable as you expected, Ben?"

Sir Benjamin raised his eyebrows slightly. "It was, old chap," he murmured. "We got along famously, didn't we, Mrs. Terrell?"

"I don't want to raise your hopes, Ben, but

the lady hasn't a bean. Don't be misled by appearances." Deliberately, his eyes lingered on the emeralds around Margaret's throat.

Margaret flushed angrily, but Sir Benjamin's good humor remained unimpaired. "Thanks for the warning, Marcus," he replied comfortably, with a rich chuckle. "But what makes you think I am hanging out for a rich wife?"

"I just wanted to keep the record straight," Mr. Salterson replied smoothly. Taking the half-finished cup from Margaret's hand, he put it on a nearby table. "This is our dance, I believe."

"What a—a thoroughly despicable man you are!" she gasped as he pulled her unwillingly into his arms. "These emeralds are a loan from Miss Salterson and have nothing to do with you!"

"They are family jewels and will eventually come to me for my wife," he said harshly. "Just don't get so fond of them that you can't give them up!"

"How—how dare you?" she whispered horrifiedly.

"I dare because you have neglected your duty, madam!" he said in a low, savage voice. "Your duty is Annabelle, and you have allowed her to dance twice with Lord Montfield! If I had not stopped it and sent her off with Mendenhall, she would have been led out onto the floor a third time by him!"

175

"Oh! No, no!" She whitened. "You are mistaken! She c-couldn't! She wouldn't!"

"I assure you she did," he replied dryly. "Girls are remarkably susceptible to rakes like Montfield. I asked my aunt how she met him, but she was unable to give me an answer. Can you?"

"I—I d-don't know. Which is Lord Montfield?"

"Right now he is in conversation with Lady Maulbrais. By the window."

"Oh." She swallowed miserably. "It was last night at the concert. A lady who claimed to know Miss Salterson brought him up to us as we were taking punch."

"And Aunt Horry knew about this?"

"N-no. Her attention was elsewhere. But I may say, sir," she rallied slightly, "I see nothing wrong with Lord Montfield. His manners were very agreeable, and he was most respectful. And of course, he is very handsome."

"He is not a person whom I wish Annabelle to know, and if you were as knowledgeable as you think you are, you would recognize him for what he is—a fortune hunter," he replied sarcastically. "You are to nip their acquaintance in the bud immediately, but I trust you not to make the mistake of running him down to Annabelle. That would merely make him more attractive in her eyes."

She nodded mutely, although she still reserved

judgment about Lord Montfield. But Annabelle had been indiscreet to dance more than once with any gentleman at a Bath Assembly Ball. The mystery was why Lord Montfield had been equally rash.

When she voiced this thought to Mr. Salterson, he replied shortly, "He is confident of his ability to charm ladies of all ages. He may have thought, too, that you were enjoying yourself too much to notice what she does, and because I have been neglectful in the past, he may have assumed that I would continue to do so. He knows better now. Don't worry, Mrs. Terrell; so long as the mantle of my protection covers both of you, you are quite safe from rogues like Montfield."

"Just Annabelle, Mr. Salterson!" she snapped. "*I* don't need you."

"I'll remember that in the future, Mrs. Terrell," he replied with cold politeness, "if you will do the same."

CHAPTER X

The following day, when Annabelle learned that her uncle had banned her friendship with Lord Montfield, she treated her aunt and Margaret to a violent temper tantrum. It ended in a stormy burst of tears, culminating in an accusation that Margaret was not, as she put it, "on her side." By the time she finally flung herself up to her room, Margaret was appalled at the scene one seventeen-year-old girl was capable of making all on her own. Miss Salterson took it more philosophically.

"We'll go out for a while and leave her to cry it out, my dear," she said, thrusting her knitting needles into her wool and putting it away. "We'll do a little shopping, perhaps buy her something pretty, and when we return, we will discover that she has recovered and is all ready to forgive and forget. You will see."

Apparently, Miss Salterson knew what she was talking about. When they returned, they found Annabelle all smiles and sweet apologies for having upset her dear Aunt Horry and her dear, dear Meg. Margaret was too grateful for the change to question it, but Miss Salterson told her later, with a puzzled expression on her face, that during their absence Lady Maulbrais had called and spent some time in the parlor with Annabelle. Perhaps the contrast had served to remind her that her uncle, whatever his faults, was preferable to her aunt, Miss Salterson added thoughtfully.

But whatever happened that day, the olive branch had been tendered and Annabelle began visiting her aunt Serena every day. Mr. Salterson was out of town for a few days on business or Margaret might have mentioned the phenomenon to him. As it was, Annabelle's friendship with her aunt caused no problems; if anything, Annabelle was more ingratiating, more eager to please.

Sir Benjamin was a frequent visitor to Camden Place while his friend was gone. In fact, either he or Lucian were found there most of the time, and Miss Salterson was of the opinion that Margaret's affairs were much more interesting than Annabelle's. She discovered that she was looking forward with anticipation to the time when Mr. Salterson returned to Bath. But not even Miss Salterson's wildest dreams could have visualized the actuality.

The first notice of his return was shortly after breakfast one morning, when he was shown into the parlor by Mulroyd, where he found Annabelle alone, dressed in her riding habit. Through narrowed eyes, he watched as expressions of dismay and uneasiness crossed her face before she masked it behind a smile.

"And where, may I ask, are you going, infant?" he asked, taking her chin between his thumb and forefinger and planting a light kiss upon her brow.

"Riding, Uncle Marcus."

"Alone?" He raised a questioning eyebrow.

"N-no. Aunt—Aunt Serena is making up a party."

"Generous Aunt Serena!" he mocked gently. "So you've patched up your differences?"

"Oh, yes. She has been most k-kind."

"And the horses? Has she brought her own stables from Queen's Keep?"

"Just one, Uncle Marcus. I borrow her mare."

"And the party she makes up? Does it ever include Sir Benjamin? Or either of the Mendenhall brothers? Or Mrs. Terrell?"

"She—t-they don't like her. She has her own

friends, Uncle Marcus." By now, Annabelle was avoiding his eyes, her face the picture of guilt.

Suddenly he dropped his bantering tone and said sternly, "I suggest you stop feeding me these lies, Annabelle! How long has your aunt been aiding you in seeing Lord Montfield?"

She stared at him in dismay, her mouth agape.

"No doubt ever since I left Bath. She would not have dared if I had been in town," he said grimly. "Do your aunt Horry and Mrs. Terrell know about this?"

She shook her head sullenly. "How did *you* know?" she asked sulkily.

"It was simple, little fool!" he spat contemptuously. "Do you imagine it would not get around that you have been seen every day on the bridle path in the company of Lord Montfield? I took steps to find out how this was possible when I left orders that you were not to see him again. I discovered from your aunt Horry's coachman that you are in the habit of visiting your aunt Serena every day, usually wearing riding clothes. How, may I inquire, did you get your talent for intrigue, Annabelle? Did you learn it from Mrs. Terrell?"

She paled slightly. "No. She isn't to blame! I— Aunt Serena said—she suggested that I visit her and see—— But why, Uncle Marcus? Monty is very agreeable, and we've done nothing wrong by meeting while in Aunt Serena's company, or in the company of her friends——"

"Did you know that the mare you have been riding belongs to Lord Montfield?" he interrupted brutally.

She hung her head.

"So you do know? And presumably your aunt knows all about it too? Surely you realize that it is improper for you to be seen riding *his* horse? That it gives rise to speculation about your relationship with him?"

"No one knew," she muttered.

"How do you know it will be kept a secret, you stupid little idiot?" he demanded bitterly. "All he has to do is tell it and your reputation's smirched. Obviously, you cannot even be allowed any freedom until you learn a few rules of conduct——"

"But, Aunt Serena said—he was a gentleman—and eligible—and you were wrong—"

"I'll have something to say to your aunt later," he replied uncompromisingly. "Meanwhile, I tell you again that you are not to have anything to do with Montfield! I do not know if your aunt does not know his true character or if she merely does not care. She has her own motives for fostering this friendship, and whatever they are, you may be sure she does not mean you well. I suspect she wants you so compromised that your reputation can be saved only by marrying Cedric. And, so far as that goes, Annabelle, life with Cedric would be heaven compared to your existence as Montfield's wife. Ten years ago he killed his first man in a duel, a husband defending his wife's honor. Since that time, Montfield has killed three others, and in every case it has been a quarrel over a woman. Do you think I want that for you? Montfield is desperately anxious to marry an heiress, and if I were not such a good marksman, he would have found an opportunity to challenge me already. Once rid of me, he would have a clear field with you. This is what happened to the brother of the last girl he ruined. She, too, was an heiress, but she did not come off so lucky in her encounter with Lord Montfield. Her guardian took her to Europe to wait out the birth of her baby."

"I don't believe you," she whispered. "It couldn't be. Ten years ago—why, he isn't old enough to——! He doesn't look old enough to——"

"My poor little girl," he said pityingly. "He is as old as I am, at least. Anyone can tell you that. Ask Sir Benjamin if you don't believe me."

Her eyes searched his face convulsively, then with a wail she flung herself into his arms. She burst into tears and he held her, patting her shoulder, until she quieted and the convulsive sobbing dwindled into an occasional, long, shuddering sigh. There was a tap at the door, and dimly, she heard Mulroyd telling her uncle that Lady Maulbrais's coachman was at the door, inquiring about Miss Annabelle.

Her uncle's reply was short and profane. "Tell him—— No, never mind, Mulroyd. I'll tell him myself!" He put Annabelle aside and strode out of the room.

When he returned from delivering a blistering message to her coachman to be given to Lady Maulbrais, he found Margaret in the parlor with Annabelle. From the books she was carrying one could deduce that she was on her way to the circulating library. She was distractingly beautiful in an amber-colored printed dimity with short sleeves, a narrow skirt, and a bodice trimmed with a double pleating of ribbon. She was wearing a chip bonnet, tied under her chin with a wide satin bow. Apparently she had been attempting to question Annabelle, who was beginning to cry afresh.

"Mr. Salterson!" She turned on him angrily as soon as he entered. "What has been going on? Did I hear you rightly? Was that Lady Maulbrais's coach you were sending away?"

"It was," he replied coolly, stung by her censuring tone. "I am serving notice on you now, Mrs. Terrell, that Annabelle is never to visit her aunt again. I hope that *this* time you will make an attempt to carry out my orders, unlike your usual slipshod methods in the past. At least until I can make arrangements for another chaperon," he added.

Annabelle gave a low moan. Margaret stiffened slightly.

"I presume you have a reason for that astounding statement?" she asked sweetly.

"I have," he replied grimly.

"And it is?"

"I think you would prefer not to know my reasons," he said sardonically. "They are too numerous, and I haven't the time to catalog them here."

She drew a sharp breath. "You must do as you please, of course," she snapped. "But I would have thought that even you would hesitate to break our agreement, quite apart from breaking Annabelle's heart and reducing her to tears."

"Annabelle's heart can take care of itself," he replied sarcastically. "But my reasons for getting rid of you can be reduced to a nutshell. You have greatly neglected your charge, and moreover, encouraged her to deceive her aunt and me! Since my aunt is fond of you, I intend to send you home with as little scandal as possible. Otherwise I might be tempted to make an example of you for serving her so treacherously."

Annabelle burst into a new spate of tears, and Margaret gasped with shock. His attack was so unexpected that at first, she was at a loss for words to repel it. But being Margaret, that unhappy state of affairs did not last long. Her temper, which she had found increasingly difficult to control in her encounters with Mr. Salterson, burgeoned alarmingly.

"I can't say that I am surprised to learn that you're capable of going back on your word," she countered in a deadly sweet voice. "You've wanted to be rid of me from the beginning! However, I refuse to allow you to accuse me of neglect, and as for deceit and—and treachery!—— No, the shoe belongs on the other foot, Mr. Salterson! *You* are treacherous to hint that I would use Miss Salterson's fondness for me to overlook my responsibilities to A-Annabelle! How dare you? *I* have not neglected her! That is *your* habit! I love Annabelle and have done everything I can to make her satisfied to be your ward! *That* was a mistake, too, but how was I to know that instead of merely being the selfish, pleasure-loving individual she thought you were, you are also an unfair, cruel, arrogant *monster?*"

She paused for breath, and he broke in. By now his anger was past the point of no return. "Oh, you've played your cards well, madam, since you learned that she was an heiress," he snarled. "You have already used her to blackmail me into allowing you to become her chaperon, and you've also managed to wheedle a valuable emerald necklace out of my aunt!" Margaret gasped with outrage, but he swept on without allowing her time for denial. "But never fear, I shan't allow you to continue your machinations! My eyes are open to your character. I think you once said something to me about heiresses and counterfeit love, didn't you?" he added smoothly. "Have you forgotten?"

Margaret felt as though a bucket of cold water had been flung into her face. By this time she was lost to all reason in her fury at the sarcastic, arrogant male animal standing before her.

"I am not surprised that you put that interpretation on my motives, or any woman's, since you are so accustomed to buying love yourself. Annabelle has told me a little something of your experiences along that line, and what a high price you pay to obtain the commodity!"

She shivered at the devil's look that came into his face. "Now I know more than ever, you are an improper person to have the care of Annabelle," he said with deceptive silkiness. "Whatever gave you the idea that the subject of my mistress was a suitable topic of conversation to hold with a seventeen-year-old girl?"

Annabelle, who had been following their quarrel with growing horror, was aghast. "No, no, Uncle Marcus! Meg didn't discuss it with me! It was I—that is, I mentioned it to Meg and she—Meg told me that I mustn't talk about such things! It was nothing like she claims. She is only trying to make you angry."

Margaret, who was by now gibbering with rage, stopped her furiously. "No, Annabelle! Don't apologize for me! Don't you dare! He is a rude, overbearing—*vulgar* man! I never said the word—— I wouldn't use such a word as—" she choked to a stop, unable to go any further.

He was watching her struggles sardonically. "Mistress?" he queried mockingly. "No, you didn't use the word, but that is what you meant, isn't it? By God, I really think you need to be taught a lesson. Twice you have flown at me like a termagant, accusing me of improprieties before my niece and my ward! If it is the last thing I do, I intend to school you in propriety! You dare to take me to task over an order! You dare to question my authority over my ward? Well, I am not disposed to go into explanations with *you*, madam! If my aunt wishes to question me, she may, but not *you!*"

What would have been the outcome of that decidedly inflammatory speech is unknown, for at that moment the door opened and Miss Salterson hurried into the room.

"Marcus! Meg! Whatever is the matter? One can hear your quarreling all over the house! The servants——" She stopped short, her eyes going from Annabelle's tear-stained face to Marcus's white-hot look of rage, then coming to rest thoughtfully upon Margaret's fiery countenance.

"Oh no, not again!" she said resignedly. "Marcus, you haven't lost your temper *again*? Meg? What is it this time? Marcus, what have you been saying to make Annabelle cry?"

Rigidly, he explained the whole story. As Margaret listened, her horror grew and her rage diminished. She was too appalled at Annabelle's narrow escape to appreciate any other viewpoint. It was not until she caught a fleeting look of self-righteousness on Mr. Salterson's face that she became aware of her own indefensible position.

"For mercy's sake, Marcus," his aunt cried in astonishment. "You knew this—this story all the time and you did not warn us? Why not?"

"It was hardly the sort of story one repeats to a woman," he replied stiffly. His anger was still simmering, but he had been slightly mollified by the look on Margaret's face.

"Why ever not?" Miss Salterson said simply. "What a refreshingly old-fashioned person you are, my boy!"

Since no one likes to be told, especially by a maiden aunt, that one possesses an antiquated viewpoint, it was not unexpected that Mr. Salterson should look disconcerted.

"No, I very much fear, my dear Marcus, that you

have become too accustomed to having your orders accepted without question. Apparently it never occurred to you to offer an explanation, yet it would have prevented all of this misunderstanding if you had simply told Margaret—or me—or even Annabelle this story, instead of merely issuing an arbitrary order and expecting it to be obeyed without a murmur. Really, if the truth were told, you owe everyone of us an apology. However, we know that you cannot help your prejudices against women, so we will endeavor to forget it and overlook your shocking lapse of conduct this time. But you must not keep us in the dark in the future about things we should know."

At first Mr. Salterson listened in offended silence, but by the end, a glint that might have been defined as humor was in his eyes.

"Aunt Horry," he finally remarked, after an obvious struggle to mask his chagrin. "How does it happen that I have ended up as the culprit? I feel somehow that I have come out of this as a darker villain than Montfield himself."

"I really couldn't say, dear boy," she replied tranquilly, "but if one loses one's temper, one is apt to say more than one should."

The two antagonists looked guiltily at one another. Mr. Salterson spoke first.

"Mrs. Terrell, I apologize. You are not to be

blamed. Of course you are not to give up your chaperon's duties," he added meticulously.

"I am at fault too, sir," she replied haltingly. "I spoke hastily and did not consider my words first. I condemned you before I gave you an opportunity to explain and——" She stopped, biting her lip. "It is my frightful temper!"

"Yes," he agreed, with a note of amusement. "Please do not say any more. You don't apologize at all well, you know. Obviously, it is painful for you, and if you continue, you may become angry again."

That night at dinner, Miss Salterson was encouraged to hope again. Guests were present, but Mr. Salterson managed to inform Mrs. Terrell privately that he did not think she would see Lady Maulbrais in Bath again. He had not been granted an opportunity to speak to her ladyship, for she had discovered a pressing reason to leave town, apparently as a result of the message she received from her coachman. So much in charity was Mr. Salterson with Mrs. Terrell that Mr. Mendenhall, who had hitherto viewed Sir Benjamin as his main rival, now switched and threw out several broad hints of inquiry as to when Mr. Salterson intended to return to London, all of which that gentleman blandly ignored.

CHAPTER XI

The following afternoon as Margaret was dressing to walk to Milsom Street to execute a few errands for Miss Salterson, she received a message that Mr. Salterson was downstairs and wished to see her. Close questioning of Mulroyd assured her that he had not asked first for her aunt or Annabelle.

After Mulroyd had proceeded on his dignified way to inform Mr. Salterson that Mrs. Terrell would be with him shortly, Margaret completed her toilet, and at the same time, made an effort to control the agitated fluttering of her breath. A tremor of nervousness assailed her, and she reminded herself sternly that it would be disastrous to allow Mr. Salterson to know that the mere fact of his presence had such an effect on her nerves. After all, they were merely tolerant acquaintances. Until yesterday, she had been indifferent to him; and yesterday, she had hated him more wildly than she ever thought it possible to hate another human being. Today, was she going to find it impossible to regard him rationally, she demanded fiercely? Leaning forward to survey herself in the mirror, she was shocked at her pale cheeks, and she pinched them viciously to bring up the color. Fortunately for her peace of mind, she was already dressed in one of her best walking dresses of mulled sarsnet, and it merely required the smoothing of her hair to be ready, else she might have dithered indefinitely.

Mr. Salterson was dressed in his usual casual, slipshod manner. His waistcoat was, as always, well-fitting across his broad shoulders, but he had thrust a number of whip thongs in the buttonhole, dragging the lapels down, and his buckskins, although of the softest and most supple leather, had been allowed to become deplorably mud-stained. As for his topboots, they looked as though they had been wrested from the hands of his valet before they were polished. His aunt would have, no doubt, viewed his appearance with a shudder, but Margaret noticed instead an absurd lock of black hair dangling in his eyes.

She explained in a stiff little voice that Annabelle

was on a day's trip, touring the Wells Cathedral, and added anxiously, in case there was some question about it, that the group was well chaperoned by two of the mothers of the young people involved and that she hoped he had no objection?

Mr. Salterson merely smiled and commented negligently that it sounded like the sort of excursion he approved of, then added in a drawling voice, "This is all very enlightening, Mrs. Terrell, but why should you think that I am here for Annabelle? I asked for you, and I have come to see if you would like to take a drive in the country in my curricle?"

Ten minutes later, he was escorting Margaret down the walk. She was as neat as a proverbial pin, with her curls confined under a fetching little bonnet of twilled silk, tied under her chin with a wide green ribbon matching the trim on her gown. Seeing her modish perfection, one would never guess that the hem of the gown had been turned once and the bonnet had been refurbished with a new bunch of daisies. Margaret was feeling a trifle light-headed, and her hand trembled as Mr. Salterson took it to steady her into the curricle.

"Jock," he informed his groom, "I don't think I'll need you again today. You may await me at the York House, and in the meantime, have a mug of ale on me." He tossed a coin to the grinning groom, then climbed up beside Margaret. She watched as he handled the reins dexterously, making the turn before the house in a neat, economical fashion.

They took a road out into the country, and as the houses dropped away, the horses settled into a comfortable trot. Mr. Salterson spoke for the first time.

"Speaking of pleasure excursions for Annabelle," he remarked casually, "I have been thinking that it might be well to get her out of Bath for a few weeks, to allow her to get over Montfield. I considered making up a party of youngsters: George Mendenhall, Freddy Warburton, and others—you, of course, would know the young ladies who have become her special friends—and taking them to my home in Scotland. Gray Shadows is very lovely this time of year. Of course, I would expect you and my aunt to accompany us, and if you like, you may bring along your son and that old nurse of his. What do you think about it?"

A number of thoughts crowded Margaret's mind at that moment, but chiefly she felt pleasure at the prospect of several uninterrupted weeks in Mr. Salterson's company. She reminded herself sternly that she was a business employee of his—that, no doubt, the purpose of this ride was to put before her this proposition and gain her views before suggesting it to Annabelle or his aunt—but she could not subdue a heady sense of delight. However, she murmured something noncommittal in a stifled little voice that Mr. Salterson seemed to take as an assent.

He reached over and picked up her hand, which had been lying in her lap.

"Calluses," he commented, fingering the tender palm. "You have worked hard, Mrs. Terrell."

The pulse beneath his fingers leaped. "Yes, yes, I—have," she said breathlessly.

He dropped the hand gently. "Why?" he asked evenly. "You are a gentlewoman. Why is it necessary?"

"Not everyone is left with a fortune of eighty thousand pounds, Mr. Salterson!" she said spiritedly. Then, "Oh, dear, I did not intend to ever mention that dreadful fortune again! Why did I not merely say that my father was an improvident man?"

He laughed. "I was not thinking of your father. I am always conscious of your widowhood when I am with you. I was, of course, wondering why your husband left you totally dependent upon your maiden estate. He was the son of a wealthy man and your son is, I believe, his uncle's heir?"

She flushed. "Then you know Lord Buckhaven?"

He maneuvered the curricle around a slow-moving hay wagon before he replied. "I have known him a long time, but not very well apparently, for I would have thought he had too much pride to allow his grandson to live in poverty. He would be severely criticized if it were generally known. As for Giles, I knew him at Oxford."

"Giles has been very kind, but Lord Buckhaven was disappointed when his son married me," she said in a muffled voice. "No—it was more than that. He was enraged! He might have become reconciled if I had had a respectable dowry, but my father's estate was entailed, and when he learned that Teresa and I had only our mother's portion, he quarreled with my father. My father had a temper, too," she added, smiling slightly. "I inherited it. Anyway, my father died from a stroke after the quarrel."

"I am sorry," he said compassionately.

"It happened while we were in Europe. The marriage was rather sudden. Lord Buckhaven would have prevented it if possible, for he was certain I was an adventuress. Or so he implied."

"Do you mean that you eloped?" he asked oddly.

She took a deep breath. "Yes, my sister and I— and Robert—fled to Europe to escape Lord Buckhaven. We had been married three weeks before he learned where we were. We remained there a year, until my sister became too ill for us to keep her with us. Then we returned. Jodie was born while we were in Rome."

He was silent for so long, digesting this startling disclosure, that she uneasily wondered if he was shocked. To admit to an elopement was a shameful confession for a properly reared girl to make. "What a tempest in a teapot!" he said disgustedly. "Surely Robert Terrell was not a minor? He was— what age?"

"Twenty-two," she murmured.

"And you were about—nineteen, I presume? Lord Buckhaven's anger, if any, should have been directed at its rightful source, his son, who was older. He was not forced into this marriage against his will, else he would not have accompanied you to Europe."

"No, Europe was Robert's idea, to avoid his father. Lord Buckhaven forgave him and would have received him back into the family if he had deserted me. He was—is—a cruel man. You say you know him, but do you know that he beat his sons until they were grown men? And his poor wife, too, while accusing her of unfaithfulness! Giles's wife was chosen for him, but he would not allow Robert and his brothers to marry, claiming that it was Giles's place to secure the succession. He was sick with a sort of possessive jealousy, wanting to keep his sons from living normal lives with wives and families. And when we returned from Europe, the two brothers between Giles and Robert had drowned in a boating accident, so it was even more important to get Robert back. At first he wanted Jodie, too, but later——" She stopped abruptly.

"That was why you eloped, then. Robert was afraid of him?"

"Yes. Robert was desperate to get away. He saw me as his salvation." Yes, there was a hesitancy, almost a withdrawing in her voice, as though she was keeping something back.

"You must have loved him very much?" he asked tentatively.

"I—don't know. He was a dear, kind person. At the last, he tried to save me from any more grief than necessary. He knew Jodie must not fall into his grandfather's hands, so he appointed my cousin and Mr. Clavering his guardians until he is twenty-one."

"Then that is why Lord Buckhaven does not support you? Because he does not have control of the boy? I am surprised he has not fought you on that issue. I would have thought, knowing his vengeful nature, he would try to take the boy away from you."

"No," she said slowly. "To do that he would have to give up taking—his revenge."

"How? The pleasure of keeping you in poverty?" He snorted. "He must be blind! He must see that, given your beauty and social standing, you will marry again someday, as most widows so. And for this dubious pleasure he stubbornly refuses the comfort of his grandson?"

She looked at him wonderingly. "Apparently you don't remember—or know, what happened to Robert? His father can't forgive me or forget it, for if he did, he would have to admit that it was his fault. You see, he sent for Robert—on business, he said. It was only a few months after our return from Europe. Robert was reluctant to go, but we were so desperately poor—with Teresa's fees and the baby's things—that he went, hoping that his father would relent and grant him an allowance or—— But instead——" She broke off. "I don't know precisely what happened, but afterwards, Robert went out to the stables, where he kept a gun in his saddlebag, and shot himself. That is why Lord Buckhaven hates me so much. That is why he hasn't spoken to me since the day of Robert's funeral."

Before Mr. Salterson could comment upon this startling disclosure, they were interrupted by the pounding hoofbeats of a horseman who was approaching them at a dead gallop. They watched curiously as the flying horse and rider from afar drew closer and they could make out the features of Freddy Warburton, frantically waving as he desperately tried to gain their attention. Mr. Salterson applied the whip to his horses and within a couple of minutes had drawn his curricle along-side the foam-flecked, heaving horse.

"Couldn't wait—" Freddy panted. "Miss Salterson said—try to find you—said where—I've been hunting down every road——"

"What's wrong?" Mr. Salterson asked sharply. "Is it my aunt?"

"No, no," Freddy shook his head violently. "It's——"

"It's Annabelle, isn't it, Freddy?" Margaret asked. "You were with the group that went to Wells. *What has happened to Annabelle?*"

"I'm sorry, Mrs. Terrell," he implored. "George said he must stay, so he sent me——"

"Freddy," Mr. Salterson said, with deadly calm. "If you do not tell me at once what has happened, I shall wring your neck."

That brought Freddy to the point as nothing else could have. Watching Margaret unhappily, he said, "It is Miss Annabelle, sir. She has been abducted."

"Go on," Mr. Salterson said steadily.

"We had just come out of the cathedral, sir, and were walking toward the Swan for our early dinner, which had been ordered in advance, when Lord Montfield joined our party." At Mr. Salterson's audible intake of breath, he added, "George didn't see him, sir. He told me later that you had forbidden her to see Montfield again, but I—I didn't know. Annabelle and I had fallen slightly behind the others, and when Montfield asked if he could speak to her a minute alone, she turned and went with him without an explanation to me. I naturally——" He stopped, and added apologetically, "Of course, she couldn't suspect anything. He seemed so reasonable and polite, and I guess—— Anyway, they walked around the corner and were hidden by the wall. They were not out of my sight more than a couple of minutes, so I was not suspicious, nor even—— My God, sir, why should I be? He is *supposed* to be a gentleman!" he added bitterly. "Then I heard the sound of a carriage starting up. Apparently it was ready and waiting. Even then, I didn't think anything—I went to look for her, and she was gone. I wasted time hunting, and then George returned. The rest of the party had gone into the Swan and sent George back for us with messages that we were holding up their dinner, and—oh, teasing messages, sir. I—I assumed, until George explained, that she'd gone willingly, but when he told me—— It was frightful!" Freddy's eyes showed the horror that had gradually grown upon him. "We began to systematically search, then, and within five minutes learned all we needed to know. There was a loiterer nearby who said that he saw a lady answering Annabelle's description entering the gentleman's carriage, and it looked as though she was being constrained!"

Margaret moaned and covered her face.

"And then, what happened?" Mr. Salterson asked grimly.

"George said I must go at once for you. He carried a message to the Swan party that Annabelle had been called home unexpectedly—"

"Thank God he kept his head," Mr. Salterson said tautly.

"Yes, sir, he did—did very well, sir." Freddy swallowed nervously. "He was going to search the roads, and I left him with all the money I had so that he could pay for information—he said he would await you at the Swan. The others will have left by now," he added wretchedly.

"Yes. I see. Very well, Freddy, get yourself a fresh horse and meet me at the York House. Perhaps you might be of some help. And hurry!"

His face was set and pale, and he did not volunteer any word on the return trip, but whipped up his horses to breathless speed. Margaret, occupied with clutching her seat in the fast-flying curricle, waited until they were slowing, at the edge of Bath, before asking in a small voice, "Do you think you can find her?"

He frowned. "Eventually," he said dryly. "If you mean before it is too late, I cannot say."

Margaret clenched her fists until the nails dug deep into the palms, drawing blood. "Please—allow me to go with you," she said in a stifled voice.

"Don't be a damn fool," he said harshly. "I want no one with me but Ben—and a brace of pistols. I would prefer not to have Freddy, but it is a lesser evil to have him along than spilling over with remorse and nerves at the White Hart, blaming himself for what happened."

"No, he's not to blame," Margaret agreed in an inaudible voice. "I am."

He said nothing, applying his concentration to taking the corners with a feather-edge to spare. From his set, graven face, she wondered if he even heard her.

Stopped before the Salterson doorway, he spoke perfunctorily. "Tell my aunt that I did not have time to see her. I depend upon you to do everything you can to calm her."

"Of course." Margaret leaped hurriedly to the ground. "Mr. Salterson," she faltered, "You will—"

"Yes?" He looked at her. "Yes, Mrs. Terrell, I will bring her back to you as quickly as possible."

He was gone, and she was left staring after him until he was out of sight. That had not been what she was going to say. She had been thinking of the pistols, and had meant to beg him to be careful when, and if, he met Lord Montfield. At any rate, she told herself dully, what did it matter? He would not be any more careful because she had asked him to, and in his present mood chafing at every delay, he was no doubt also cursing her incompetence and neglect, which had allowed this to happen.

CHAPTER XII

It was nearly midnight before Margaret and Miss Salterson were granted any news. They were still up, having been obliged to act as normally as possible while quieting Pendleton's fears and making up a story that would explain Annabelle's absence to satisfy the others. Miss Salterson had not been a trial to Margaret, but had behaved with typical restraint and the good manners of a true aristocrat. "She would go to the guillotine without a hair out of place," Margaret thought, wistfully as she watched the old lady quietly tatting lace by candlelight. Her bobbin, flashing in and out, had a hypnotic effect on Margaret, who had behaved very badly by Salterson standards. She had paced the floor and finally had to excuse herself when scalding tears of fear and self-reproach threatened to overcome her. Now the tears were drained away, and she felt as empty and limp as a husk. Her thoughts were miserably chaotic, allowing her no peace, for her wish to have Annabelle found in time warred with her fear that while doing so Mr. Salterson would meet with a fatal accident.

A carriage rumbled to a stop before the door. Margaret heard it first and raced downstairs to fling open the door before the knocker sounded. Annabelle threw herself into her arms, sobbing and laughing.

"Meg, don't cry so, darling. I am all right. Aunt Horry, I am here!"

Margaret's eyes went convulsively past her shoulders to George, Freddy, and Lucian, who were crowding into the doorway.

"Where is your uncle?" she asked, and Miss Salterson echoed, "Yes, where is Marcus?"

"He stayed in Wells with Sir Benjamin," Annabelle replied in an odd voice.

Miss Salterson led the way to the drawing room while a babble of voices tried to tell what happened. Finally, Annabelle was allowed her say while Miss Salterson rang for port.

"Where Monty was concerned, I have been frightfully gullible," she said humbly. "Even after Uncle Marcus explained what he was, I still had no conception of his evil. I soon learned." She shuddered. "When he asked to speak to me, I thought I owed him a chance to present his case and hear my answer in person, and when he led me around the corner, I thought he merely wanted privacy. I was a fool! Instead, he and that man-servant of his forced me into the carriage. Inside, the windows were curtained so that no one could see my struggles, and Monty soon had me gagged and tied. After we were in the country, he removed the gag and promised me that no matter how much I screamed, no one could hear. When we got to that dreadful place, Monty locked me in the attic. There was no way to escape, for there was a sheer drop of three floors to the ground below. Also, the w-window was stuck! I nearly stifled, for there was no air, nothing but a bare attic floor, and I thought I—I might be left there in that horrid e-empty place forever!"

"Miss Annabelle has been a heroine," Freddy declared, looking at her admiringly. "She hasn't cried at all, and any other girl would be having hysterics by now."

Naturally, with praise like this, the threatened breakdown was bitten back, and Annabelle continued bracingly, "I tried to talk him into ransoming me, but he said that was no good. He could never remain in England and spend the money, and he had no intention of leaving! He wanted a legal marriage. I thought then—what a fool he was, not to bother to learn that my uncle had to approve of my husband before he would release my money into his custody. But I was the foolish one. Later, I had all afternoon to reason it out. He would not allow Uncle to live long after our marriage—any man who would do what he was doing would not hesitate to have Uncle murdered. And then I would inherit all, Uncle Marcus's fortune as well as my own. I knew then," she gulped, "that he would kill me, too, and I determined that I would never marry him."

Lucian nodded. "Mr. Salterson, of course, had already figured that out long before we rescued Miss Annabelle. He did not think Montfield would —ravish her, as he did that other poor girl he abducted. For one thing, the other girl had gone with him willingly—until he killed her brother. He said that Montfield would have learned from that mistake. He would hold out for marriage—either by drugging her or bribing some defrocked parson—and then proceed to murder them both at his leisure."

"How did you find her so quickly?"

"That is why Mr. Salterson wanted Sir Benjamin, and how I happened to join the rescue party." Lucian grinned. "He and I were dining together when Mr. Salterson reached him, and perforce had to take me, too. You see, the other girl was held captive near Wells when the family found her. Her guardian, who was a friend of Sir Benjamin's, had mentioned the location of the house at one time, and Mr. Salterson hoped he would be able to find it, although it would have taken much longer without the help of some clues George was able to provide us with when we got there." He rumpled his younger brother's hair affectionately. "It was an easy matter to surprise Montfield and his servant, for they were quietly getting drunk in the kitchen when we crept up on them. They gave up without a struggle."

"Where is Mr. Salterson?" Margaret asked bluntly. "Why isn't he here?" She thought she had shrieked the words, but apparently her voice was normal enough to the others.

The men looked at one another uneasily.

"He's going to fight him, isn't he?" she asked calmly.

"It—it isn't a subject to discuss——" began George hesitantly.

"Don't be a fool, George," she said crisply. "What is the purpose of hiding the truth at this stage? After tonight, how can you be stuffy? Of course he is going to duel Lord Montfield. That has been obvious from the start. That is why he and Sir Benjamin remained in Wells, isn't it?"

"Yes, ma'am." Lucian and Freddy remained stubbornly silent. "He is to fight him at dawn. He has given Lord Montfield an ultimatum: either fight or leave this country forever. I think his lordship will fight—and shoot to kill."

Lucian, with a swift look at the ladies, rose abruptly and suggested that it was time that they left. Miss Salterson, who had been watching Margaret, agreed briskly.

Putting aside her lace, she rose too, and said, "I think we all need to go to bed. I am sure that graceless nephew of mine will turn up early in the morning looking absolutely pleased with himself. Come, Annabelle."

Shepherding Annabelle and the two younger men ahead of her, she left the room, leaving Margaret alone with Lucian. By now, Margaret had admitted to herself what should have been obvious hours before: she was in love with Marcus Salterson, and if he died, life would not be worth living. If he came out of this duel alive, she was still going to have to face a lonely, unendurable existence, but bad as it was, she would not have to live with the additional agony of knowing that he was dead through her own negligence.

"Lucian. Would you grant me a favor, my friend?" She had no idea that her eyes and face mirrored her thoughts as though they were written there.

He smiled sadly. "Just name it, Meg."

"Would you take me home? And, Lucian—I wish

to leave in time to get to that dueling spot before dawn."

When Mr. Salterson presented himself in his aunt's sitting room at ten o'clock that morning, she had had less than two hours' sleep and had been waiting for news since dawn. Although he was wearing fresh linen and was clean shaven, he looked weary; but in her overwrought condition, she flung herself at him and burst into tears. He was touched.

"Were you hurt?" she sobbed. "I know all about the duel, so you needn't bother denying it," she added waspishly, applying her handkerchief to her eyes.

He grinned. "No, Aunt Horry. I was fortunate, although it was a near miss. Montfield's aim was slightly off. He seemed nervous this morning."

"Is he—dead?"

"His right hand is shattered and may have to be amputated," he said briefly. "He'll never fight another duel, which may put an end to his amorous exploits, I should think," he added reflectively.

"Oh!"

"Aunt Horry, what would you have me do?" he asked harshly. "He tried his damnedest to kill me! I was determined to put an end to his career of rape and murder." His face took on a satanic look.

"He learned what it meant to tamper with someone belonging to Marcus Salterson."

"Y-yes, of course."

"Aunt Horry, where is Margaret Terrell? Mulroyd said she left before dawn, bag and baggage."

"She asked Lucian to take her home. They were going by Wells first, to learn the outcome of the duel." She bit her lips. "Did you not see her?"

He frowned slightly. "The surgeon mentioned another carriage parked in the lane. But no—I did not see her. Why did she leave?"

"She blamed herself for everything that happened. That is, for Annabelle continuing to see Lord Montfield."

"She is not to blame," he said shortly. "I am."

"I could just scream!" Miss Salterson burst out, blowing her nose vigorously on a minute scrap of lace and linen. "The first girl—the only girl—I have *ever* thought would suit you and look what has happened! Just as things looked promising, this wretched duel had to crop up and she must fly home, full of guilt because she thinks she caused it!"

He smiled slightly. "Aunt Horry, were you playing matchmaker?"

"Don't you laugh, Marcus Salterson!" she snapped, although he showed no indication of doing so. "I am in such a state that I don't think I shall

213

ever get over this night! I am too old to live through another month like this past one, and so far as *you* are concerned, it is precisely as Margaret said, you are bad-tempered and selfish! And moreover, you haven't an ounce of consideration for any of us!"

He gave a hoot of laughter. "Aunt Horry, I love you! Don't worry, I shall go to Chedworth and persuade her to come back. I must say, I am getting rather weary of traveling that road, however."

She eyed him hopefully, but he answered her unasked question with a mocking smile. "We mustn't have Mrs. Terrell feeling guilty over something that is not her fault, must we?" He paused on his way out. "By the way, how is Annabelle? Has she recovered from her abduction yesterday?"

She smiled ironically. "Oh yes, quite," she said dryly. "She took matters in her own hands when she learned that Margaret was gone, and persuaded George Mendenhall to hire a chaise and accompany her to Chedworth, vowing she was going to bring Margaret back. Mercy, but that boy is besotted with her!"

Mr. Salterson laughed appreciatively. "Give her another year or so, Aunt Horry, and she will be a *femme terrible!*"

Mr. Salterson was settling his bill at the York House when he was told uneasily by the clerk that a certain gentleman was waiting to see him and had been waiting for some time.

It was Lord Buckhaven, who came forward eagerly.

"Shall we go to my room, my lord?" he asked shortly.

"No, no, Salterson. I've rented a house nearby. We can easily walk there, and it will be worth your while, I guarantee ye!" he added, as Mr. Salterson visibly hesitated. "I suppose ye're wondering why I'm here? And why I want to talk to ye? Irene Marshbanks told me this is where I'd fine ye. Irene's a cousin of mine, ye know."

"Indeed?"

"Irene tried to warn me the boy—my son Robert —was falling in love with a girl in the village, the daughter of the local squire. She felt responsible because they met in her home. Netherwood. I got the message too late to stop it. They eloped, ye know."

Mr. Salterson said nothing.

"Irene seems to think ye're here to make the gal yer mistress. But I don't believe it. Doesn't make sense. You want to marry her."

By now, they were walking rapidly down the street, but at this, Mr. Salterson stopped abruptly and faced his lordship angrily. "She is mistaken, sir!" he said icily.

Lord Buckhaven hooted. "I know it!" He

snorted. "Didn't I just say I didn't believe her? Why d'ye think I came so quickly? As soon as I received the message ye'd followed her here? Brought Giles with me, so the silly fool could see for himself! He tried to tell me ye're giving the woman a carte blanche, some foolish business about a bracelet, but he and Irene don't know yer type of man like *I* do! Too proud to install a woman ye expect to make as yer mistress in yer aunt's house! Too much pride! A man like ye doesn't approach his mistress at a village tea party, either! No, it is marriage ye have in mind, and I'm here to stop it!"

"And just how do you propose to do that?" Mr. Salterson asked grimly.

Lord Buckhaven chuckled hoarsely. He looked like some predatory bird with his sharply defined face, carved with grim lines of cruelty and evil, thrust forward, and his cloak flapping behind him.

"Oh, not by forbidding the banns. I've no control over *her!* She gets no allowance from me for herself or the brat. Not that a man with yer brass would care for that! No, but I shall show ye something ye won't like, and I can promise ye, yer pride won't permit ye to marry her, then!"

"And why should that matter to you?"

"Because I hate her," was the simple reply. "She killed my son. Oh, not by pulling the trigger. Robert committed suicide. But she married him, then made his life a hell so he couldn't live any longer. I swore then I'd get even with her, and by God, I will do it! Any way I can!"

"You have no objection, however, to her becoming my mistress?" Mr. Salterson asked dryly.

Lord Buckhaven snorted. "I can't prevent it even if I wished to. But why should I mind the world knowing what a scheming hussy my son married? Easy! Available to any man with the right price! But marriage—to a flyer like ye? I'll move heaven and earth first!"

By now they had reached the lodgings Lord Buckhaven had let. They were typical of lodgings to be found in Bath. There were no servants about as Lord Buckhaven led him toward a study which was located on the ground floor of the house. Giles, also, was not in sight, nor was the elusive Mrs. Marshbanks. Lord Buchanan removed a key from his pocket, and unlocking a drawer, drew forth a paper. He paused, eyeing it gloatingly, before leaning forward and spreading it carefully before Mr. Salterson. He retained his fingertips on its edges, however, as though it were too precious to be out of his possession.

"Read it!" he rasped commandingly.

It was a simple declaration, written and signed by Robert Terrell and dated four years earlier, admitting that the child, Jodie Terrell, who was known as his son, was not, in fact, his child and therefore not entitled to any of the benefits that would normally be his by birthright. He had married Margaret Stedbelow, he wrote, knowing that the child was to be born and knowing that the child was not his. There was no force involved on her part, nor trickery nor coercion practiced. He had voluntarily agreed to marry her, in order to give the boy a name. At the same time, he added, there had been two living brothers between him and the heir to his father's title. Now, however, he and the child known as Jodie Terrell stood directly in line as his brother Giles's heirs, and he made this statement so that a fraud would not be perpetrated by allowing the child to inherit as his son. Moreover, he agreed that this statement was to be preserved among his father's papers in case at some future date Jodie Terrell attempted to claim the title. The signature was shakily executed.

Mr. Salterson looked up. The old man was watching him eagerly. "Why did your son write this?" he asked impassively.

"Why?" Lord Buckhaven sputtered. "Because I forced him to! I knew there had to be a reason for that hasty marriage, so I had the records searched in Rome and discovered that the baby was born prematurely. I taxed him with it until he broke down and confessed that the child wasn't his! Then I forced him to sign that confession so the succession would be clear. He had no choice!"

"But you are not really interested in the succession, are you? That wasn't the reason you had him sign this document. You wanted it so you could punish Margaret Terrell, didn't you?"

The old man cackled. "I told her at the funeral that she and that brat of hers would pay for the rest of their lives! That I'd use this if I ever learned another man was interested in marrying her! I've kept her in poverty—she'll die in poverty!"

"I see. What is your price for this document?"

"Price?" Lord Buckhaven's face was ludicrous. "But I—I don't wish to *sell* it, man! I thought ye'd understand that I merely want ye to *see* it!"

"Five thousand pounds." Mr. Salterson coolly pulled forward a sheet of paper and took a pen from the ink standish. "I will give you a voucher for five thousand pounds."

"Keep yer voucher!" Lord Buckhaven snarled. "Are ye still hot for that wench after what I've just shown ye?"

"Ten thousand pounds? Frankly, my lord," Mr. Salterson added contemptuously, "I wouldn't let that paper make a penny's worth of difference if I intended to marry her, and neither would any other man worth his salt."

"Does that mean ye *don't* intend to marry her?" the old man asked eagerly.

Mr. Salterson did not reply. "Will you sell it to me for ten thousand pounds?"

"No!" screamed the furious old man. "Not for ten times that! Get out! Ye're another fool, like Robert! Get out, I tell ye!" Shaking with rage, he pointed to the door.

Mr. Salterson fixed him with a steely eye that halted his upraised haind. "I will bid you good day, my lord, since I find the air in here a trifle polluted for my nostrils," he said coldly. He turned and sauntered out without haste while the old man danced with rage and slammed the door behind him.

Mr. Salterson had almost reached York House when he was halted by the sound of running footsteps behind him. Turning, he saw Giles Terrell, who came panting up to him.

"Marcus! Here!" He thrust the document Lord Buckhaven had shown him earlier at him. "I have brought you Robert's statement. I took it away from my father, by force. He is an old man and I— I was the stronger. For once. He had no right to show you or anybody else this vile thing. I was ashamed when I learned what he intended to do, so I stayed out of the way. But I can't allow this— this brutality to go on any longer toward Margaret. She is blameless. She would never put the boy forward as my heir, I know that, but—but—she doesn't deserve this," he added jerkily.

"Why are you giving it to me?"

220

"Because I heard you try to buy it, and I knew you would do what is necessary to correct this wrong. It should never have been written, you know, and wouldn't have if my father hadn't forced it out of Robert. I am sure he did not tell you that Robert went out to the stables immediately afterward and blew his brains out. From remorse, I'd say. When my father speaks of blaming Margaret, he knows who is really to blame. He was the one who made Robert's life hell," Giles added bleakly, "as he has all of our lives. My brothers' as well as mine and my mother's. I would not object to the boy being my heir," he added slowly, "for it would bring new blood into the strain, and God knows, we need it. I will never have a son, you see. My wife is ten years older than I and—but no matter. My cousin who is to inherit the title is as dissolute and rakehell as will satisfy even my father's noble ambitions!" he added bitterly.

Mr. Salterson folded the document and placed it in his breast pocket. "I said I would give ten thousand pounds for it, you know," he said slowly.

Giles flushed. "I am not a damned merchant, Salterson! It is not for sale!"

Mr. Salterson nodded and proceeded on his way. At the entrance to York House he was halted by a feminine voice calling his name. It was Irene Marshbanks. She was in an open phaeton and had apparently been waiting for him. A hat ornamented with costly ostrich feathers perched atop her head, and her silk carriage-dress of burnt orange rustled as she leaned forward eagerly.

"Did he talk to you?" she asked excitedly. "Did Lord Buckhaven tell you about *her?* About the boy? That he was a bastard? I wanted to tell you the other night that she had had a lover—perhaps more than one—before Robert, but Lord Buckhaven would not have approved of it."

"I suggest that you never allow those particular words to ever pass your lips again, Mrs. Marshbanks," he said coolly. "If so, I shall advise Mrs. Terrell to institute a suit for slander that will strip you of every penny you have."

She drew back, literally hissing like a snake. "So you don't care! You'll take her, bitch that she is! I was right—you do intend to offer her a carte blanche! As for suing me, she can't, for I can *prove* what I say!"

A hard smile touched his lips. "No, you can't, madam. Your proof is here." He tapped his breast pocket.

"He couldn't have—— He would *never* give it to you!" She sounded baffled. "Unless—unless he thought you could do a better job of destroying her." Her eyes narrowed.

"You must curb your tendency to speak out of

turn. And whatever your private opinion may be, remember, you have no proof."

And baffled, incredulous, mortified, and angry, she watched him turn and enter the threshold of York House.

CHAPTER XIII

Mr. Salterson was delayed in leaving in good time, so that he had to break his journey by spending the night on the road, midway between Bath and the village of Chedworth. He was driving his curricle and was reduced once more to the rough-and-ready ministering of Jock as combined valet, groom, and coachman. When Bench had uttered an inarticulate protest at being left behind, he had been informed curtly, "I am perfectly capable of putting on my own shirt and tying my own neck-tie!" As if that were not insult enough, he had added, "Here is money to settle the bill. If I have not returned by tomorrow at noon, hire a post chaise and bring Pendleton, yourself, and the luggage to London."

The innkeeper of the Rose-and-Crown in Chedworth greeted him as though he was an old friend, and when Mr. Salterson finally emerged after a noonday lunch to stroll toward Mulberry Cottage, he was hailed by the vicar, who was standing on the other side of the tumbled stone wall of the churchyard.

"Have you come to see my church?"

Mr. Salterson stared at him blankly. "Ah? It is Mr. Clavering, isn't it? I would like very much to see your church."

The vicar beamed and his white hair glowed like a halo in the bright sunlight. "Come in, come in." He bustled forward, delightedly prepared to act as a guide around the twelfth-century church.

Mr. Salterson, however, stopped him before he could begin. "Mr. Clavering, I would rather talk to you about Margaret Terrell."

"Ah?" The vicar's smile flickered momentarily. "Then, let's go into the garden and have a glass of cider."

There was a table set under the apple tree in the garden, but Mr. Salterson was in no mood to appreciate its rustic appeal.

"Let's cut rope, Vicar," he said bluntly. "Have done with evasions. I know about Jodie Terrell."

The vicar blinked, his face taking on the look of

a worried cherub. "I gather, then, that Irene Marshbanks made good her threat to disclose her not-so-closely-guarded secret?"

"Indirectly, yes." Mr. Salterson stirred restlessly. "I have come here, sir, with the purpose of asking Margaret Terrell to marry me, in spite of what I have been told about her. But—I must admit that I am shaken. I gather," he added, with a fair imitation of the vicar's dry voice, "that you know all about it?"

"Oh, yes. Meg told me before they were married, or she would have never allowed me to perform the wedding ceremony."

"*You* performed it? I thought——"

"Oh no, my dear boy, no. They were married right here in Chedworth before they left for Europe. It has been a well-kept secret, for Meg fears reprisals against me from Lord Buckhaven. He holds considerable influence in the church, you see."

Mr. Salterson kicked viciously at a fallen apple.

"I advised her to marry Robert," the vicar went on tranquilly. "The situation was desperate, and he was very much in love with her. She, too, felt a great tenderness for him. And Teresa, even then, was showing signs of mental instability. You *do* know about Teresa?" he added hastily.

Mr. Salterson nodded. "So, for the use of his

name," he said bitterly, "she in turn gave him a 'great tenderness'?"

The vicar watched him alertly. "She was half out of her mind with worry about Teresa, poor child. And with keeping the knowledge of Teresa's condition from her father. You must not forget Teresa if you wish to understand Meg. I presume you *do* wish to understand Meg?" the vicar asked insistently. "Sir John took advantage of Meg's good nature and sense of responsibility, to saddle her with the care of her twin. Teresa was always easily led, sensitive, gentle—— When they turned eighteen, they were both beautiful girls. Teresa fell in love, and it was Meg who strongly urged her father to agree to the betrothal."

"Betrothal?" Salterson asked absently.

"Yes. Teresa found her young man first. His name was David, and his regiment was stationed at Little Mitford. I forget which regiment—an old man's memory, you know," he added apologetically. "It was sent to Waterloo. The couple wanted to be married before he left, and Meg begged Sir John to consent, but he was adamant that there must be a waiting period. How wise his decision was is questionable, but he had heard the rumors of a battle forming at Waterloo, and he did not want his daughter widowed at the outset of her marriage."

"And the boy never came back?"

"No. News eventually filtered through to Teresa from brother officers that he had been killed. He had no immediate family, and she was probably his only mourner. Her grief was unrestrained. I—we all—feared for her reason."

"So that was why she accompanied her sister to Europe?" he asked curiously. "I wondered."

"Yes." Mr. Clavering seemed on the verge of adding something more, for Mr. Salterson could see the words almost trembling on his lips, but he closed his mouth grimly and substituted, "I think Lord Buckhaven must be a little mad. A result of his own parentage, no doubt. The sins of the fathers visited upon the children." He shook his head sadly. "Robert once told me a little of his father's history. He was the only son of sadistic parents: his only value to them was as his father's heir. His mother paraded a series of lovers through her bedroom before the child, and the father was no better. He was a member of an infamous club similar to the Mohawks. The child was alternately abused by his parents and fawned upon by the servants, and loved by no one. When he, in turn, had children, he became extremely possessive of them since they represented the only love he had ever known."

Mr. Salterson shrugged. "Buckhaven's story is not a unique one, Vicar," he said dryly. "It has happened before. A married woman has many lovers, perhaps even bears a child fathered by one of them. In some cases the lover might also be a friend of the husband. The husband is indifferent. So long as the succession is taken care of, how many marriages then become a matter of convenience for both parties? If a wife is discreet, many husbands do not care what she does."

The vicar sighed. "And so the rot is perpetuated unto the second, even unto the third generation."

Mr. Salterson hardly seemed to hear him. He was staring vacantly across the churchyard, where Polly and Annabelle, with Jodie between them, were approaching the village. Polly had a market basket over her arm. Bidding the vicar a hasty, abrupt farewell, Mr. Salterson made his departure.

Meanwhile, Margaret was alone at Mulberry Cottage. She had known when Annabelle made her unexpected appearance yesterday that Mr. Salterson would not be far behind. It had not been her choice to see him again, and she did not minimize the pain she would feel when she had to say a final good-bye to him, but she was determined to act in as dignified and normal a manner as possible.

She had not expected to see him again after Lucian's carriage pulled away from the little woodland copse near Wells. It had been an agonizing decision—to watch the duel—but she could not leave until she knew the outcome. Once the men took their places, she fixed her eyes convulsively upon Lord Montfield, for she could not bear to see Mr. Salterson receive a bullet in his flesh. She saw his lordship, in what seemed an unbearably long length of time, raise his arm, deliberately take aim, and fire. The ten seconds that followed were another lifetime, until Lucian's whisper, "He missed!" freed her to look again and see Lord Montfield receive the shattering impact of a bullet in his right hand. He was wearing a look of shocked surprise as he fell.

Then, she had looked at Mr. Salterson. He was still standing erect, pale but otherwise unhurt, and she had promptly slid into a swoon. When she had come to, the carriage was moving. Her emotion was obvious to Lucian, who said very little but was surprisingly tender and gentle on the homeward trip, considering that he was witnessing the death of his own hopes to win Margaret Terrell. Why, she had thought achingly, was she fated to be loved by good, kind men and to love in turn a black-browed brute who despised and distrusted her? Why, oh why, couldn't she love Lucian Mendenhall instead of Marcus Salterson, she had asked herself despairingly.

She was outside, struggling to mend the fence of the goose pen, when she looked up to find him watching her, having apparently followed the sounds of hammering to the back of the house. To her chagrin, a deep flush overspread her face.

"Let me do that," he said gravely, taking the hammer from her hands.

"A fox got in last night," she said hopelessly, watching him deal competently with the gate. "Annabelle is here," she added.

"Yes, I know." He bent over the gate. "I wanted to talk to you alone first."

"Were you hurt?" she asked indistinctly.

"Hurt?"

"In the duel."

"Oh. No, I wasn't touched. Montfield's aim was off. But surely you were there?" He pounded the pickets in place with short, quick strokes.

"Yes, I was there. But I—didn't see all of the end. When I—left, you were still standing, but I wasn't sure. I couldn't—know." She was agitated.

He glanced quickly at her but said nothing more. When he finished, she led him through the kitchen and into the little parlor. She had whipped off her apron on the way, and she lowered her sleeves and smoothed her cuffs before facing him primly.

"I would like to take my niece back to London today, Mrs. Terrell. How soon can she be ready?"

Margaret quivered slightly. He was wasting no time; it was now mid-afternoon, and they would not arrive in London until nearly dusk. Was it then so urgent? "Right away, I think," she answered composedly, "as soon as she returns. If you'd like, I'll go upstairs and get her things ready now."

"No. Leave it. I wish to talk to you first. Do you recognize this?"

He did not, like Lord Buckhaven, keep his hands on it, but handed it to her. She took it wonderingly. A deep flush spread over her face when she read the first line.

"I never read it, but I know what it is. Lord Buckhaven told me at the funeral that he had it. He said he would use it if Jodie ever tried to become a contender for——" She stopped, her mouth working. She laid the paper carefully down upon the table beside her, her hand trembling. Her body seemed diminished somehow, shrinking as though expecting a blow. He had wanted her humiliated once, had sworn to accomplish it, but this hurt unbearably.

"I can imagine what Lord Buckhaven said," he replied roughly. "I suggest you use that tinder box beside you and burn that at once."

"How did you come by it?"

"Giles wrested it from his father and sent it to you."

"I see. Giles is—generous. Is that why you are removing Annabelle from this house so quickly?"

He hesitated. "Is the document incorrect, then?"

She picked it up and read it through, then slowly lit one corner of it with a spark from the tinder box. It flared up, and she dropped it into the fireplace and watched it burn to ashes. When she turned around, her face was pale and stern.

"No," she said thoughtfully. "No, so far as it goes, it is quite true. I'll get Annabelle's things ready for her now."

He stopped her. "Can you explain it to me?"

"Robert Terrell was a very kind person. He was not like his father. He never reproached me because I couldn't love him."

"You used him then?" he asked bitterly.

"Yes." She faced him squarely. "You might say that. But he didn't care, he was happy with me. When we returned to England, he arranged for Teresa to go to Dr. Stockton's hospital. All would have been well if his father—— But no doubt, Robert felt an obligation to his father's heir."

"Mrs. Terrell," he said abruptly, "will you marry me?"

"Why?" She stared at him dazedly. "Why are you asking me now? After that?" She indicated the charred embers in the fireplace.

"It is because of that," he said dispassionately. "Lord Buckhaven won't stop merely because he no longer has that paper. He may even try to take the boy away from you. You need protection from the slanders that will be hurled at you by both him and Mrs. Marshbanks. As my wife, my mantle will fall over you and your son. No one will dare repeat a word Lord Buckhaven might say. As for your neighbor, her mouth will be effectively closed. Then, there is your son. He has no future to look forward to now unless you can marry a man who is willing to provide for him. Not many will be, you know."

"Mr. Salterson, you astonish me," she said with a shaky little laugh. "Are you always this charitable?"

He did not pretend to misunderstand her. "Oh, I am not asking you for altruistic motives, if that is what you mean. I merely wish to point out the advantages from your point of view." He laughed shortly. "From mine, I admit that I want you most damnably, and what I want, I get, one way or another. I know that you had other proposals. Ben, for one, told me he got nowhere. And there is Mendenhall. But you have refused them both, and I understand now why. Because of the boy? You won't marry any man unless you first tell him about the boy?"

She nodded.

"I suppose Jodie's father deserted you and Robert Terrell kindly came to your aid? And you went to Europe to disguise the date of his birth? I don't really wish to know the details," he added hurriedly. "The less I know, the better. I am still prepared to marry you in spite of it, I assure you of that. At first, I admit that I did think of a carte blanche, but I knew that you were a virtuous woman in spite of what happened to you in your past."

"You would have, then, offered me— That is, if you had had the slightest idea I would accept it, you would have asked me to become your mistress?" she asked in a low, trembling voice.

"Perhaps. I don't know. You see, I am trying to be absolutely honest. I don't think I would, however. I don't really want anything temporary. And marriage seems the best safeguard for permanency. I will explain," he added sternly, and the condemnation in his voice was directed as much at himself as at her for all that it made her cringe. "I don't intend for this to be a *modern* marriage. I will not expect to have another mistress any more than I will expect you to have another lover."

"In that case, why are you taking Annabelle away from my house?"

"Annabelle?" Mr. Salterson was surprised at what seemed to him a frivolous change of subject. "You must see, surely, that I cannot allow her to remain. I shall arrange to find a respectable woman to act as her chaperon, and put her in her own establishment——"

"Your wife—would not be respectable enough?"

He frowned. "As soon as Annabelle marries," he said crisply, "she will be allowed to visit us and you to visit her, but until then——"

"Until then, I am not good enough for her? Mr. Salterson, will you be good enough to get out of my house?" Margaret's voice was shaking.

He was shocked to see that she was angry at what he considered a sane, sensible discussion of marriage. Her face was paper white, her eyes black, and she was trembling so violently that she had to grip a chair-back to keep from falling.

"Meg," he said quickly, in an appeasing voice, "perhaps I worded myself awkwardly, but surely you see why—— You must be aware that Lord Buckhaven will continue to talk, aren't you? I can protect your reputation; indeed, as a married woman, his talk won't harm you, but an unmarried young girl like Annabelle——"

"No, I don't see, Mr. Salterson, and I am not Meg to *you!*" The tears were rolling down her cheeks, tears of anger that she dashed away impatiently. "I don't see how you would wish to have a wife who would not be good enough for your niece. If so, she shouldn't be your wife." He started to speak, but her voice rose. "I wonder too, sir, if you have given any thought to children? Since you say that your proposal is motivated by feelings of lust, then I assume there might be children? Will they, too, be removed from the corrupting influence of their mother? Concede the awkwardness of such a situation, Mr. Salterson. Far better to make me your mistress and have done with it!" she added ironically. "I am, however, merely speculating, for the matter will never be put to a test. You have confessed to such feelings of hesitancy that I am sure you will be relieved, in the end, that I am declining your gracious proposal of marriage. By the time you arrive in London, you will have overcome any slight feelings of disappointment you might have in having your suit rejected, I am sure. As for me, I shall have no difficulty whatsoever in accepting *my* good fortune! In fact, sir," she hissed between gritted teeth, "I would prefer not to have to wallow in gratitude for the rest of my life because you did me the favor of of marrying me!"

"That is enough!" he snapped, feeling thoroughly offended as well as injured. "You are angry, naturally, and like a woman, incapable of looking at the matter rationally. I would have thought you would exercise a little honesty——"

"Honesty?" she cried furiously. "You call that proposal honest? You make it clear to me that you have proposed only because you have a desire to lie with me——"

"It is you who became pregnant out of wedlock, Mrs. Terrell," he said coldly, "and no amount of twisted thinking can change *that* fact. I have not blamed you for it, and had no intention of ever referring to it again after marriage, but——"

"But you had no intention of forgetting it either!" she snapped. "And everything you have said shows that you are thinking of it. Oh no, Mr. Salterson, I don't want that kind of life! I would rather accept a carte blanche from *any* man I know than be married to *you!*"

"I see that I was wrong in expecting to deal in truths with you." He was now as angry as she was. "You want pretty language——"

"Never from you!" she screamed. "Not one word of love—only lust, and condemnation, and—and insults!"

"That's enough, you shrew!" he shouted, storming toward the door. "My offer of marriage is withdrawn!"

"That's fine with me!" she screeched, pulling open the door so hard that it struck the wall and bounced back. "Get out of my house, and stay out! Forever! If you ever return, *ever,* I shall notify the magistrate to arrest you! *Mr. Lucian Mendenhall!*" she added for good measure.

At the front door he ran straight into Annabelle, who was coming through it with George. Polly was behind them, holding Jodie's hand.

"Annabelle," he snapped, "get your clothes! We are leaving!"

CHAPTER XIV

As soon as they had gone, Margaret fled to her bedroom and indulged in a storm of weeping that lasted until nightfall. She was deaf to Jodie's frightened calls and Polly's repeated poundings on the locked door. Her life was over, she told herself passionately. Now that it was too late, now that he had come and gone for the last time, she admitted that she would have given anything—her soul, almost—to have had his proposal made in such a way that she could have accepted it. How could she be so weak, she thought, hating herself. His proposal of marriage had been no better than a carte blanche. But, oh God, this pain and longing that clawed at her, mangling her heart and her pride—how soon would it go away? How she longed for peace and a mindless state of contentment. How she envied old Polly, who seemed past all the unholy desires of the flesh and body! She desperately wished for her state of mind before she had met Marcus Salterson; for her former calm, rational self.

Annabelle had treated him to a magnificent tantrum when she realized that he meant that he was taking her away forever, and Annabelle in the full tide of a tantrum was awesome for all of her mere seventeen years. Mr. Salterson was too furious to reason with her, and Salterson vs. Salterson had been something to see. Or to hear, for Margaret had remained behind the closed parlor door. She gained a certain grim pleasure in thinking of the ride back to London; he could not enjoy it. In the end, Polly had been the one to gather the girl's things together while Annabelle ran in to kiss her good-bye and promise fiercely, "Don't worry. I shall be back!" Before Margaret could remind her that she must be cautious—that her uncle now held the whip in hand and would not hesitate to wield it—they were gone.

Margaret glared at herself in the mirror and put away her wet towel. It was time to forget Marcus Salterson, she said stormily, time to forget a dark, mocking face and an intelligence that perfectly matched her own. Time to forget Annabelle, too. She could not afford to indulge herself by longing for what she could not have. She had to work to live. The fruit was ripe, with the jelly to be made. A thousand tasks, neglected for too long, beckoned her.

Accordingly, she was in the garden the following afternoon when she looked up to see Mr. Salterson strolling out of her kitchen door as unconcernedly as though she had not threatened to have him evicted the day before. She was standing on a kitchen chair, reaching to the topmost branches of the apple tree, while Polly held a wooden bowl and Jodie romped nearby with his puppy. It was very hot, unseasonably so, and Margaret's face was damp and shiny, with ringlets clinging to her neck and forehead. She was dressed in her oldest dress, which was much too tight for her, and she had unbuttoned the top buttons for coolness. A little rivulet of perspiration trickled down her throat between her swelling breasts and Margaret, gazing at Mr. Salterson between her upraised arms, saw an unmistakable look of naked desire leap like a flame into his eyes as he returned her smoldering look.

He said nothing, however. He merely waited with a disturbing smile for the outcry that he was obviously expecting, and when it came, it was in a voice that would have frozen an icicle.

"What do you want?" Margaret demanded. "How *dare* you return to my house?"

He was dressed, she saw, as though he was paying an important town call, in a dark blue coat of superfine and cream-colored pantaloons that clung to his strong legs and thighs as though molded to them. Not a lock of hair was out of place for the first time since she had met him. She had never seen him looking so correct, but she was ignorant of the fact that he had arrived at the Rose-and-Crown with not only his valet, but sufficient luggage to do justice to his appearance.

His answer was mild in the face of her hostility. "This morning, Annabelle's maid awakened me to tell me that her jewel case was missing. She had not unpacked her portmanteau until earlier this morning, so she did not discover the loss before then. I assumed she has left it here."

"Impossible," Margaret said crisply, leaping lightly to the ground. "All of Annabelle's things are gone from the room she shared with me. You left it in the carriage."

"No, the only thing Annabelle had was the portmanteau, and I personally handed that to Pendleton when we arrived." He was smiling ruefully as he met her eyes, as though he was amused. It seemed a puzzling reaction to the loss of thousands of pounds in jewels, thought Margaret angrily.

"Then Pendleton is lying," Margaret snapped, frowning at him. "It isn't here."

"Miss Meg," Polly half-whispered, "I packed that portmanteau myself. The jewel case wasn't in it. I—I didn't see it in her room and thought she had it with her."

"That is what happened! She carried the jewel case into the house herself!" Margaret said angrily. "Why do you jump to the conclusion that *we* have it before you ask Annabelle about it?"

"Pendleton awakened Annabelle and questioned her about it before she came to me," he replied in the same mild, reasonable voice. "She said if the box was not in the portmanteau, she left it here. Pray disabuse your mind of the thought that I am accusing you of stealing the jewels. I assume they were left accidentally, and I am merely asking you to look for them."

"Oh, very well," she said irritably. She turned and led the way through the kitchen and into the tiny entry hall. This time, she did not ask him into the parlor. "Wait here. We will find your niece's jewel case as quickly as possible, Mr. Salterson, and then I hope you will leave at once and never return. Polly, come with me."

He nodded meekly. Jodie was standing in the door, watching him with big, round eyes, and Mr. Salterson selected a coin from his pocket and sent him to the village bakery for a gingerbread man. Overhead, he could hear the scraping sound of furniture being moved and her raised, agitated voice as Polly apparently protested something. He went into the little parlor, and seating himself leisurely, waited. A minute later, Margaret appeared in the doorway. Her face was stormy, and she was thoroughly ruffled. Behind her, Polly's face was white and fearful.

"There has been a mistake," she snapped.

He rose slowly.

"Your Pendleton is in error." She faced him with icy composure, her voice scornful. "The jewel case is not here. I don't know what you hope to gain by these accusations against us, but——"

"It is you who are in error," he said positively. "Pendleton does not make mistakes. She has been caring for those jewels since my sister was a girl. If she says the jewel case is not there, it is not there."

"Oh, Miss Meg," Polly's moan was horrified, "he is a wicked, wicked man. He means to have me arrested for stealing, to punish you——"

"He will do no such thing," Margaret blazed. "What is your purpose in this trumped-up story, sir? If you think I will allow you to punish old Polly merely to intimidate me—to gain your point that I am unworthy of you—" she choked.

He considered her speculatively, then looked at

Polly. "Get out!" he said sharply. "Get out and leave me alone with her! And stop blubbering, old woman!" he added in a rough voice that reassured her at once. "I shan't arrest you even if we never find the silly jewels. Now, get out!"

"Yes, sir!" Polly scampered out, laughing.

"What do you mean by ordering my servant about?" Margaret demanded smolderingly. "*I* shall not allow you to drop the investigation! *I* shall insist on your bringing the constable here to search! I intend to *prove* that those jewels are not here! I don't know what you expect to gain by this despicable, *low* maneuver——"

"Merely this." He moved quickly, before she could guess his intention, and jerked her into his arms and kissed her. Instantly, she was fighting him in a wild attempt to break free, but he merely tightened his arms until she could not move. Then he kissed her again, and this time, he took his time and the kiss was very thorough. When he raised his head, he was breathing hard, and was holding in his arms a trembling, frightened woman.

"How dare you, sir?" she gasped weakly. "I hate you——" He silenced her at once with another long, lingering kiss. Thereafter, he did not allow her to gasp out more than a word or two before stopping her in the same effective manner. Finally, she was silent. He waited mockingly.

"Well?" he murmured provocatively, his eyebrows raised.

"I shan't speak until you release me, sir," she gritted. "Unhand me!"

"No doubt," he agreed teasingly. "But I shan't release you so long as you are this angry. It has finally occurred to me, my love, that we cannot speak together without coming to fisticuffs, so that I am better off beginning at the end and working backward. If I had done this yesterday instead of proposing, I would not have been so quickly in hot water."

"You were in hot water, as you say, sir, because of the nature of your proposal, not because you didn't kiss me——"

"No. Hush!" He kissed her again briefly. "I was appalled when I thought back on what I said yesterday. How you managed to endure me long enough to order me out of the house I cannot guess. My arrogance, my conceit, in imagining that by offering you my name I could dare make rules——! I cannot look back upon it without shuddering. I am ashamed to remember what I said. The only excuse I can offer is that I have been thrown off balance for days. I have never been in love before, and I find the experience extremely unsteadying."

She was at least listening, he saw with a surge

of relief. Standing within the circle of his arms, she was listening.

"Nothing has changed," she said coldly. "I am still what I am. I am still unfit for Annabelle."

His arms tightened slightly, but even so, her breath was cut off. "And that was the cruelest cut of all. I was vile! How could I mention— No, listen, love," his voice deepened. "I want to explain. As you say, you haven't changed. No, thank God. You are still beautiful Meg Stedbelow who had a child out of wedlock and became Meg Terrell, and have lived a cruel existence ever since. Whatever you did—without even knowing how it happened—I know you were innocent of any wrongdoing, that you were then, as you are now, completely moral in your behavior, because you are you! When I realized that, I changed and it was a revelation! I saw it all last night and knew that I had lost you through my stupidity and blindness. You would never, I knew, allow me close enough to you again to tell you so."

Her eyes—they were navy-blue today—were watching him steadily.

"Then this morning, Pendleton came to see me about the missing jewels, and I saw, with relief, that I had a lever to get into this house again. I have used it shamelessly, I admit, my darling, but I was a desperate man. My love," he whispered into her ear, "will you listen to me now?"

Her head was bent, but he caught a movement that might have been a nod.

"You are kind, loyal, generous, tender—and I would be the happiest man on earth if you would honor me by becoming my wife. Annabelle is desolate at being parted from you. Will you and Jodie, even old Polly, come to me?"

She looked, her eyes brimming with joyous laughter. "What about the jewels?"

He grinned. "Blast the jewels! I have suspected the truth about them from the beginning. I think they are hidden somewhere in the house."

"Hidden? Not by me?" Margaret cried sharply.

"No," he agreed, his grin widening. "By Annabelle, with young George's help, of course. He showed up in London this morning just before I left. I suspect the two of them are on their way here right now. The whole thing must have been planned between them within a matter of minutes," he added admiringly, "which shows some fast thinking, since at the same time Annabelle was throwing hysterics."

"But what if you are wrong?" Margaret fretted. "And they have been stolen——?"

"Will you stop borrowing trouble, my sweet?" he scolded gently. "I refuse to believe that I am wrong, but I don't care if the silly jewels are never found, since they have served their purpose. Of far more interest to me is the fact that you have not yet answered my proposal, and I am becoming anxious. Will you forgive me and marry me?"

Instead of answering, Margaret smiled at him. "Obviously, you haven't seen the vicar today?"

Puzzled by the change of subject but reassured by her smile, he replied slowly, "No. I saw him yesterday, but today—no. Why?"

"Because he was here yesterday while I was— unhappy. He said then that he intended to tell you about Jodie. I have never told anyone but the vicar the truth. He knows about Teresa and Robert and the reason for our marriage. He said it was unfair to you—to both of us—to keep the truth from you any longer. But oh, Marcus, you came to me without knowing and you said you didn't care," she added triumphantly.

"But, dear heart," he said patiently, with infinite tenderness, "I already know the truth. Don't you remember? And—I—don't—care!"

Her nose wrinkled mischievously. "You were marvelous, wonderful, but you don't know the truth. Only that Robert and I were married to give Jodie a name. You see, Jodie is not my baby. He is Teresa's. Her fiancé was killed at Waterloo, and Teresa was pregnant. Then—she became ill, from the grief and shame and fear. She accompanied us to Rome where, in strange surroundings, it was easy to pass Jodie off as my and Robert's child."

She had to stop then to be kissed repeatedly,

and in between kisses, Marcus muttered in a stunned whisper, "I am a fool! A blind fool! Forgive me, darling."

"A doctor in Rome told us about Dr. Stockton. As soon as Jodie and Teresa could travel, we brought them back to England and put her in Lawton Grange. And—oh, Marcus, she is well! Dr. Stockton writes that they are going to be married and—she—wants Jodie back. Dr. Stockton wants to adopt him."

His eyes searched her face anxiously. "How do you feel about that?"

She smiled bravely. "Sad. Happy. But as Dr. Stockton's son, he will be safe from Lord Buckhaven. Don't you think that is reason enough to let him go?"

He hugged her fiercely. "Jodie is ours, but we may let her have him part of the time," he declared. "Why didn't I guess the truth? God knows, I had enough hints—enough clues!"

"I shall never forget that you proposed beautifully, before you knew," she said tranquilly.

"Yes, after insulting you in every possible way," he groaned.

"No, I won't allow you to say that!" This time, she used his own method of silencing him and when she drew back, his eyes were twinkling.

"I am a very lucky man to be judged by your kinder standards," he teased. "I suppose Robert knew about Teresa when he offered to marry you?"

"Yes. He was a friend of David's and, when he died, suspected what was wrong even before I did. I was almost crazy with worry. I couldn't tell my father, with her pleading with me not to. Oh, Robert was marvelous. He thought of it all. The planning—everything. Poor boy, he tried so hard! He was so good." Her eyes filled with tears.

"Yes. He was a wonderful man. I shall always be grateful to him," Marcus agreed, cupping her rosy face in his hand and studying it tenderly.

So absorbed were they in themselves that they did not hear the front door knocker, the door opening, and then the sound of hushed breathing in the doorway.

"Oh! George!" A delighted whisper alerted them to the presence of watchers. "This is better than anything I hoped for! I don't know what I was expecting—at best, a toleration of one another, but this—this is *love!*"

Margaret jumped and Mr. Salterson looked up, flushing. Annabelle was surveying them triumphantly, her head on one side, her funny little face with its wide, toothy smile all eagerness. She was dressed in a dashing creation of bronze silk, and upon her head was one of the new upstanding poke bonnets. It was fashioned of twilled velvet, tied with an enormous satin ribbon beneath her chin. The famous Salterson nose was twitching with curiosity.

Directly behind her, grinning and shuffling his feet sheepishly, was George Mendenhall, in an unaccustomed high collar and flowing tie.

"You two were lost to the world," Annabelle said innocently. "George and I knocked and knocked, and since we were unable to arouse a soul, we walked on in. And what do we find? You two cuddling and cooing! You can't kiss Meg unless you are going to marry her, Uncle Marcus. Are you going to marry her?"

"Annabelle," her uncle said in a dangerous voice, "what did you do with that jewelry box?"

She gurgled. "How long did it take before you tumbled to the truth?"

"I did it, sir," George said bashfully. "Annabelle thrust it at me in the kitchen, so I hid it in the chicken coop while Polly was packing her things and you and she were shouting."

"The chicken coop! What a splendid idea, George!" Margaret cried admiringly.

"You haven't answered my question, Uncle Marcus," Annabelle said. "Are you going to marry Meg?"

"It occurs to me, my child, that although I have asked her repeatedly, she has not yet answered me. So, if you two will remove yourselves to the hen-house and recover your property—and close the door behind you—" The door closed with a resounding bang. "Now, my darling," he turned to Margaret. "I demand an answer this time. *Will you marry me?*"

Dell Bestsellers

At your local bookstore or use this handy coupon for ordering: